Sashenka Part One

St Petersburg, 1916

Simon Montefiore

W F HOWES LTD

This large print edition published in 2008 by
W F Howes Ltd
Unit 4, Rearsby Business Park, Gaddesby Lane,
Rearsby, Leicester LE7 4YH

1 3 5 7 9 10 8 6 4 2

First published in the United Kingdom in 2008
by Bantam Press

The author and publishers are grateful for permission to reproduce
the following copyright material: for 'The Talisman', from *Pushkin*
by Henri Troyat, translated by Nancy Aphoux, © 1970 by
Doubleday, a Division of Random House Inc. Used by permission
of Doubleday, a division of Random House Inc.; for lines from
Lady Macbeth of Mtsensk by Nikolai Leskov, translated by Robert
Chandler © Robert Chandler, 2003. Reprinted by permission of
Hesperus Press; for the song of Petrograd street children, quoted
with permission from *The Silver Samovar: Reminiscences of the
Russian Revolution*, Alexander Poliakoff (Atlantida Press). Every
effort has been made to obtain the necessary permissions with
reference to copyright material. We apologize for any omissions
in this respect and will be pleased to make the appropriate
acknowledgements in any future edition.

A CIP catalogue record for this book is available
from the British Library

ISBN 978 1 40742 705 8

Typeset by Palimpsest Book Production Limited,
Grangemouth, Stirlingshire
Printed and bound in Great Britain
by MPG Books Ltd, Bodmin, Cornwall

To Santa

There where the waves spray
The feet of solitary reefs . . .
A loving enchantress
Gave me her talisman.
She told me with tenderness:
You must not lose it,
Its power is infallible,
Love gave it to you.
Alexander Pushkin, 'The Talisman'

Now and again in these parts, you come across people so remarkable that, no matter how much time has passed since you met them, it is impossible to recall them without your heart trembling.
Nikolai Leskov, *Lady Macbeth of Mtsensk*

Here I am abandoned, an orphan, with no one to look after me, And I will die before long and there'll be no one to pray at my grave, Only the nightingale will sing sometimes on the nearest tree . . .
Song of Petrograd street children, 1917

CHAPTER 1

It was only teatime but the sun had already set when three of the Tsar's gendarmes took up positions at the gates of the Smolny Institute for Noble Girls. The end of term at the finest girls' boarding school in St Petersburg was no place for policemen but there they were, unmistakable in their smart navy-blue tunics with white trimming, shiny sabres, and lambskin helmets with sultan-spikes. One clicked his fingers impatiently, another opened and closed the leather holster of his Mauser revolver and the third stood stolidly, legs wide, with his thumbs stuck into his belt. Behind them waited a traffic jam of horse-drawn sleighs, emblazoned gold and crimson with family crests, and a couple of gleaming limousines. The slow, slanting snowfall was visible only in the flickering halo of streetlights and the amber lamps of touring cars.

It was the third winter of the Great War and it seemed the darkest and the longest so far. Through the black gates, down the paved avenue, the white splendour of the pillared Institute rose out of the early twilight like an ocean liner adrift in the mist.

Even this boarding school, of which the Empress herself was patron and which was filled with the daughters of aristocrats and war profiteers, could no longer feed its girls or heat its dormitories. Term was ending prematurely. The shortages had reached even the rich. Few could now afford the kerosene to run a car, and horsepower was fashionable again.

The winter darkness in wartime St Petersburg had a sticky arctic gloom all of its own. The feathery snow muffled the sounds of horses and engines but the burning cold made the smells sharper: petroleum, horse dung, the alcohol on the breath of the snoring postilions, the acrid cologne and cigarettes of chauffeurs in yellow- and red-trimmed uniforms, and the flowery scents on the throats of the waiting women.

Inside the burgundy leather compartment of a Delaunay-Belleville landaulet, a serious young woman with a heart-shaped face sat with an English novel on her lap, lit by a naphtha lamp. Audrey Lewis – Mrs Lewis to her employers and Lala to her beloved charge – was cold. She pulled the bushy lambskin up over her lap; her hands were gloved, and she wore a wolf-fur hat and a thick coat. But still she shivered. She ignored the driver, Pantameilion, when he climbed into his seat, flicking his cigarette into the snow. Her brown eyes never left the door of the school.

'Hurry up, Sashenka!' Lala muttered to herself in English. She checked the brass clock set into the glass division that kept the chauffeur at bay. 'Not long now!'

A maternal glow of anticipation spread across her chest: she imagined Sashenka's long-limbed figure running towards her across the snow. Few mothers picked up their children from the Smolny Institute, and almost no fathers. But Lala, the governess, always collected Sashenka.

Just a few minutes, my child, she thought; my adorable, clever, solemn child.

The lanterns shining through the delicate tracery of ice on the dim car windows bore her away to her childhood home in Pegsdon, a village in Hertfordshire. She had not seen England for six years and she wondered if she would ever see her family again. But if she had stayed there, she would never have known her darling Sashenka. Six years ago, she had accepted a position in the household of Baron and Baroness Zeitlin and a new life in the Russian capital, St Petersburg. Six years ago, a young girl in a sailor suit had greeted her coolly, examined her searchingly and then offered the Englishwoman her hand, as if presenting a bouquet. The new governess spoke scarcely a word of Russian but she knelt on one knee and enclosed that small hot hand in her own palms. The girl, at first hesitantly then with growing pressure, leaned against her, finally laying her head on Lala's shoulder.

'*Mne zavout Mrs Lewis*', said the Englishwoman in bad Russian.

'Greetings to a bespoke guest, Lala! I am be-named Sashenka,' replied the child in appalling English. And that had been that: Mrs Lewis was henceforth 'be-named' Lala. The need met the moment. They loved each other on sight.

'It's two minutes to five,' said the chauffeur tinnily through the speaking tube.

The governess sat forward, unhooked her own speaking tube and spoke into the brass cup in excellent Russian (though with an English into-nation). 'Thank you, Pantameilion.'

'What are the pharaohs doing here?' said the driver. Everyone used the slang term for the polit-ical police, the Gendarmerie. He chuckled. 'Maybe the schoolgirls are hiding German codes in their petticoats?'

Lala was not going to discuss such matters with a chauffeur. 'Pantameilion, I'll need you to come in and get her trunk,' she said sternly. But why were the gendarmes there? she wondered.

The girls always came out on time. Madame Buxhoeven, the headmistress, known to the girls as Grand-maman, ran the Institute like a Prussian barracks – but in French. Lala knew that Grand-maman was a favourite of the Dowager Empress Maria Fyodorovna and the reigning Empress Alexandra.

A cavalry officer and a gaggle of schoolboys and students in gold-buttoned uniforms and caps walked through the gates to meet their sweet-hearts. In Russia, even schoolboys had uniforms.

4

When they saw the three gendarmes, they started, then walked on, glancing back: what were the political police doing at a boarding school for noble girls?

Waiting to convey their masters' daughters home, the coachmen, in ankle-length padded robes lined with thick white lamb's fur, red sashes and bowler hats, stamped their feet and attended to their horses. They too observed the gendarmes.

Five o'clock. The double doors of the Smolny swung open, casting a ribbon of canary light down the steps towards the gates.

'Ah, here they come!' Lala tossed her book aside.

At the top of the steps, Madame Buxhoeven, severe in her black cape, serge dress and high white collar, appeared in the tent of light – as if on wheels like a sentry on a Swiss clock, thought Lala. Grandmaman's mottled bosom, as broad as an escarpment, was visible even at this distance – and her ringing soprano could crack ice at a hundred paces. Even though it was freezing, Lala pulled down her window and peered out, excitement rising. She thought of Sashenka's favourite tea awaiting her in the little salon, and the biscuits she had bought specially from the English Shop on the Embankment. The tin of Huntley & Palmers was perched beside her on the burgundy leather seat.

The coachmen clambered up on to their creaking conveyances and settled themselves, whips in hand. Pantameilion pulled on a beribboned cap and jacket trimmed in scarlet and gold and, stroking a well-waxed moustache, winked at Lala. Why do men expect us to fall in love with them just because they can start a motor car? Lala wondered, as the engine chugged, spluttered and burst into life.

Pantameilion smiled, revealing a mouthful of rotten fangs. His voice came breathily through the speaking tube. 'So where's our little fox then! Soon I'll have two beauties in the car.'

Lala shook her head. 'Hurry now, Pantameilion. A trunk and a valise, both marked Aspreys of London. *Bistro!* Quick!'

CHAPTER 2

It was the last class: sewing for the Tsar and Motherland. Sashenka pretended to stitch the khaki breeches but she could not concentrate and kept pricking her thumb. The bell was about to ring, releasing her and the other girls from their eighteenth-century prison with its draughty dormitories, echoing refectories and alabaster ballrooms.

Sashenka decided that she would be the first to curtsy to the teacher – and therefore first out of the classroom. She always wanted to be different: either the first or the last but never in the middle. So she sat at the very front, nearest the door.

She felt she had grown out of the Smolny. Sashenka had more serious matters on her mind than the follies and frivolities of the other schoolgirls in what she called the Institute for Noble Imbeciles. They talked of nothing but the steps of obscure dances, the cotillion, the *pas d'espagne*, the *pas de patineur*, the trignonne and the chiconne, their latest love letters from Misha or Nikolasha in the Guards, the modern style for balldresses and, most particularly, how to present their décolletage. They discussed this endlessly with Sashenka after lights-out because she had the fullest breasts in her class. They said they envied her so much! Their shallowness not only appalled but embarrassed her because, unlike the others, she had no wish to flaunt her breasts.

Sashenka was sixteen and, she reminded herself, no longer a girl. She loathed her school uniform: her plain white dress made of cotton and muslin with its twee pinafore and a starched shoulder cape, which made her look young and innocent. Now she was a woman, and a woman with a mission. Yet despite her secrets, she could not help but crave her darling Lala waiting outside in her father's landaulet with the English biscuits on the back seat.

The staccato clap of 'Maman' Sokolov (all the teachers had to be addressed as Maman) broke into Sashenka's daydreams. Short and lumpy with fuzzy hair, Maman boomed in her resounding bass: 'Ladies, time to collect up your sewing! I hope you have worked well for our brave soldiers, who are sacrificing their lives for our Motherland and his Imperial Majesty the Emperor!'

That day, sewing for Tsar and Motherland had meant attaching a newfangled luxury – zippers – to breeches for Russia's long-suffering peasant conscripts, who were being slaughtered in their thousands under Nicholas II's command. This task inspired much breathless giggling among the schoolgirls.

'Take special care,' Maman Sokolov had warned, 'with this sensitive work. A badly sewn zipper could in itself be an added peril for the Russian warrior already beset by danger.'

'Is it where he keeps his rifle?' Sashenka had whispered to the girl next to her. The other girls had heard her and laughed. None of them was sewing very carefully.

The day seemed interminable: leaden hours had passed since breakfast in the main hall – and the obligatory curtsy to the huge canvas of the Emperor's mother, the Dowager Empress Maria Fyodorovna with her gimlet eyes and shrewish mouth.

Once the ill-zippered trousers were collected, Maman Sokolov again clapped her hands. 'A minute until the bell. Before you go, *mes enfants*, I want the best curtsy of the term! And a good curtsy is a . . .'

'LOW curtsy!' cried the girls, laughing.

'Oh yes, my noble ladies. For the curtsy, *mes enfants*, LOW is for NOBLE GIRLS. You'll notice that the higher a lady stands on the Table of Ranks granted to us by the first emperor, Peter the Great, the LOWER she curtsies when she is presented to Their Imperial Majesties. Hit the floor!' When she said 'low', Maman Sokolov's voice plunged to ever more profound depths. 'Shopgirls make a little curtsy *comme ça* –' and she did a little dip, at which Sashenka caught the eyes of the others and tried to conceal a smile – 'but LADIES GO

9

LOWWWWWW! Touch the ground with your knees, girls, *comme ça –*' and Maman Sokolov curtsied with surprising energy, so low that her crossed knees almost touched the wooden floor. 'Who's first?'

'Me!' Sashenka was already up, holding her engraved calf-leather case and her canvas bag of books. She was so keen to leave that she gave the lowest and most aristocratic curtsy she had ever managed, lower even than the one she had given to the Dowager Empress on St Catherine's Day. '*Merci, maman!*' she said. Behind her she heard the girls whisper in surprise, for she was usually the rebel of the class. But she did not care any more. Not since the summer. The secrets of those hazy summer nights had shattered and recast everything.

The bell was ringing and Sashenka was already in the corridor. She looked around at its high moulded ceilings, shining parquet and the electric glare of the chandeliers. She was quite alone.

Her satchel – engraved in gold with her full name, Baroness Alexandra Zeitlin – was over her shoulder but her most treasured possession was in her hands: an ugly canvas book bag that she hugged to her breast. In it were precious volumes of Zola's realist novels, Nekrasov's bleak poetry and the passionate defiance of Mayakovsky.

She started to run down the corridor towards Grand-maman, who was silhouetted against the lamps of limousines and the press of governesses and coachmen, all waiting to collect the Noble Young Ladies of the Smolny. But it was too late. The doors along the corridor burst open and suddenly it was flooded with laughing girls in white dresses with white lacy pinafores, white stockings and soft white shoes. Like an avalanche of powdery snow, they flowed down the corridor towards the cloakrooms. Coming the other way, the herd of heavy-hoofed coachmen, their long beards white with hoarfrost and bearing the freezing northern night in their cloaks, trudged forward to collect the girls' trunks. Resplendent in his flashy uniform with its peaked cap, Pantameilion stood among them, staring at Sashenka as if in a trance.

'Pantameilion!'

'Oh, Mademoiselle Zeitlin!' He shook himself and reddened.

What could have embarrassed the ladykiller of the servants' quarters? she wondered, smiling at him. 'Yes, it's me. My trunk and valise are in Dormitory 12, by the window. Wait a minute – is that a new uniform?'

'Yes, mademoiselle.'

'Who designed it?'

'Your mother, Baroness Zeitlin,' he called after her as he lumbered up the stairs to the dormitories.

What had he been staring at, Sashenka asked herself: was it her horrible bosom or her over-wide mouth? She turned uneasily towards the cloakroom. After all, what was appearance? The shallow realm of schoolgirls! Appearance was nothing compared to history, art, progress and fate. She smiled to herself, mocking her mother's scarlet and gold taste: Pantameilion's garish uniform made it obvious that the Zeitlins were nouveaux riches.

Sashenka was first into the cloakroom. Filled with the silky furs of animals, brown, golden and white, coats, *shapkas* and stoles with the faces of snow-foxes and mink, the room seemed to be breathing like the forests of Siberia. She pulled on her fur coat, wrapped her white fox stole around her neck and the white Orenburg shawl around her head and was already heading for the door when the other girls poured in, home-bound, their faces flushed and smiling. They threw down shoes, slipped on little boots and galoshes, unclipped leather satchels and bundled themselves into fur coats, all the time chattering, chattering.

'Captain de Pahlen's back from the front. He's paying a visit to Mama and Papa but I know he's coming to see me,' said little Countess Elena to her wide-eyed companions. 'He's written me a letter.'

Sashenka was almost out of the room when she heard several girls calling to her. Where was she going, why was she in such a hurry, couldn't she wait for them, what was she doing later? If you're reading, can we read poetry with you? Please, Sashenka!

The end-of-term crowd was already pushing, shoving through the door. A schoolgirl cursed a sweating old coachman who, carrying a trunk, had trodden on her foot. Freezing outside, it was feverishly hot in the hall. Yet even here Sashenka felt herself quite separate, surrounded by an invisible barrier that no one could cross, as she heaved her canvas bag, coarse against the lushness of her furs, over her shoulder. She thought she could feel the different books inside – the anthologies of Blok and Balmont, the novels of Anatole France and Victor Hugo.

'Mademoiselle Zeitlin! Enjoy your holidays!' Grand-maman, half blocking the doorway, declared fruitily. Sashenka managed a *merci* and a curtsy (not low enough to impress Maman Sokolov). Finally, she was outside.

The biting air refreshed and cleansed her, burning her lungs deliciously as the oblique snow nipped her cheeks. The lamps of the cars and carriages created a theatre of light twenty feet high but no more. Above her, the savage, boundless sky was Petrograd black, tempered with specks of white.

'The landaulet is over there!' Pantameilion, bearing an Asprey travelling trunk over his shoulder and a crocodile-skin valise in his hand, gestured across the drive. Sashenka pushed through the crowd towards the car. She knew that, whatever happened – war, revolution or apocalypse – her Lala would be waiting with her Huntley

13

& Palmers biscuits, and maybe even an English ginger cake. And soon she would see her papa too.

When a valet dropped his bags, she leaped over them. When the way was blocked by a hulking Rolls with a grand-ducal crest on its glossy flank, Sashenka simply opened the door, jumped in and climbed out the other side.

Engines chortled and groaned, horns hooted, horses whinnied and stamped their hooves, servants tottered under pyramids of trunks and cases, and cursing coachmen and chauffeurs tried to find a route through the traffic, pedestrians and grimy ice. It was as though an army was breaking camp, but it was an army commanded by generals in white pinafores, chinchilla stoles and mink coats.

'Sashenka! Over here!' Lala was standing on the car's running-board, waving frantically.

'Lala! I'm coming home! I'm free!' For a moment, Sashenka forgot that she was a serious woman with a mission in life and no time for fripperies or sentimentality. She threw herself into Lala's arms and then into the car, inhaling its reassuring aroma of treated leather and the Englishwoman's floral perfume. 'Where are the biscuits?'

'On the seat, darling! You've survived the term!' said Lala, hugging her tightly. 'You've grown so much! I can't wait to get you home. Everything's ready in the little salon: scones, ginger cake and tea. Now you can have the Huntley & Palmers.'

But just as she opened her arms to release Sashenka, a shadow fell across her face.

'Alexandra Samuilovna Zeitlin?' A gendarme stood on either side of the car door.

'Yes,' said Sashenka. She felt a little dizzy suddenly.

'Come with us,' said one of the gendarmes. He was standing so close that she could see the pores of his pockmarked skin and the hairs of his ginger moustache. 'Now!'

CHAPTER 3

'Are you arresting me?' asked Sashenka slowly, looking round.

'We ask the questions, miss,' snapped the other gendarme, who had sour milky breath and a forked Poincaré beard.

'Wait!' pleaded Lala. 'She's a schoolgirl. What can you want with her? You must be mistaken, surely?' But they were already leading Sashenka towards a plain sleigh parked to one side.

'Ask *her* if you want to know,' the gendarme called over his shoulder, gripping Sashenka tightly. 'Go on, you tell her, you silly little bitch. You know why.'

'I don't know, Lala! I'm so sorry! Tell Papa!' Sashenka cried before they pushed her into the back of the sleigh.

The coachman, also in uniform, cracked his whip. The gendarmes climbed in after her.

Out of sight of her governess, she turned to the officer with the beard. 'What took you so long?' she asked. 'I've been expecting you for some time.' She had been preparing these lines for the inevitable moment of her arrest, but annoyingly the policemen did not seem to have heard her as the horses lurched forward.

Sashenka's heart was pounding in her ears as the sleigh flew across the snow, right past the Taurida Palace and towards the centre of the city. The winter streets were quiet, swaddled by the snow. Squeezed between the padded shoulders of the two gendarmes, she sat back, enveloped in the warmth of these servants of the Autocrat. Before her, Nevsky Prospect was jammed with sleighs and horses, a few cars, and trams that clattered and sparked down the middle of the street. The gas streetlamps, lit day and night in winter, glowed like pink halos in the falling snow. She looked past the officers: she wanted to be seen by someone she knew! Surely some of her mother's friends would spot her as they came out of the shops in the arcades of Gostiny Dvor, the Merchant's Row bazaar with its folksy Russian clutter – icons, stuffed bears and samovars.

Flickering lanterns and electric bulbs in the vast facades of the ministries, ochre palaces and glittering shops of Tsar Peter's city rushed past her. There was the Passazh with her mother's favourite shops: the English Shop with its Pears soap and tweed jackets, Druce's with its English furniture, Brocard's with its French colognes. Playful snowflakes twisted in a little whirlwind, and she hugged herself. She was nervous, she decided, not frightened. She had been put on earth to live this adventure: it was her vocation.

Where are they taking me? she wondered. The Department of Police on Fontanka? But then the sleigh turned fast on Garden Street, past the forbidding Mikhailovsky Castle where the nobles had murdered the mad Tsar Paul. Now the towers of the Peter and Paul Fortress rose through the gloom. Was she to be buried alive in the Trubetskoy Bastion? But then they were heading over the Liteiny Bridge.

The river was dark except for the lights hung across the bridges and the lamps of the embankment. As they crossed, she leaned to her left so she could look at her beloved St Petersburg just as Peter the Great had built it: the Winter Palace, the Admiralty, Prince Menshikov's Palace and, somewhere in the gloom, the Bronze Horseman.

I love you, Piter, she thought. The Tsar had just changed the city's name to Petrograd because St Petersburg was too German – but to the natives it was always St Petersburg, or just Piter. Piter, I may never, ever see you again! Adieu, native city, adieu Papa, adieu Lala!

She quoted one of Ibsen's heroes: *All or nothing!* This was her motto – and always would be.

And then there it was: the drear dark-red brick of the Kresty Prison, looming up until its shadows swallowed her. For a moment the great walls towered over the little sleigh as the gates swung open and then clanged shut behind her.

Not so much a building, more of a tomb.

CHAPTER 4

The Delaunay-Belleville careered down Suvorovsky and Nevsky Prospects with Pantameilion at the wheel, and pulled up outside the Zeitlin family house, a Gothic façade of Finnish granite and ochre, on Bolshaya Morskaya or Greater Maritime Street. Weeping, Lala opened the front door into a hall with a checkered floor, almost falling on to three girls who, with cloths tied to their hands and knees, were polishing the stone on all fours.

'Hey, your boots are filthy!' howled Luda the parlourmaid.

Lala's shoes left melted slush on the gleaming floors but she did not care. 'Is the baron at home?' she asked. One of the girls nodded sulkily. 'And the baroness?'

The girl glanced upstairs and rolled her eyes – and Lala, trying not to slip on the damp stone, ran to the study door. It was open.

A mechanical sound like the shunt of a loco-motive came from inside.

Delphine, the surly and ancient French cook, was getting her menu approved. A wife would normally take care of such matters – but not in this uneasy house, as Lala was well aware. The colour of a wax candle, as thin as a broomstick, Delphine always had a drip on the end of her long nose, which hung perilously over the dishes. Lala remembered Sashenka's fascination with it. What happens if it falls into the borscht? she'd ask, her grey eyes sparkling.

'They don't help you, *mon baron*,' the cook was saying, haggard in her creased brown uniform. 'I'll talk to them if you like, sort them out.'

'Thank you, Delphine,' said Baron Zeitlin. 'Come in, Mrs Lewis!' The cook stood up straight like a birch tree, stiffened proudly and passed the nanny without a glance.

Inside the baron's study, Lala could savour the leather and cigars even in her tears. Dark and lined with walnut, the room was crammed with expensive clutter and lit by electric lights in flounced green shades. Palms seemed to sprout up every wall. Portraits suspended on chains from the ceiling looked down on sculpted heads, small figurines in frock coats and top hats, and signed sepia photographs of the Emperor and various Grand Dukes. Ivory fans, camels and elephants mingled with oval cameos lined up on a baize card table.

Baron Samuil Zeitlin was sitting in a strange contraption that shook rhythmically like a trotting horse as he manipulated its polished steel arms, his hands on the wooden handles, his cheeks slightly red, a cigar stub between his teeth. The Trotting Chair was designed to move the baronial bowels after meals.

'What is it, Mrs Lewis? What's happened?'

Trying not to sob, she told him, and he jumped straight off the Trotting Chair. Lala noticed that his hands were shaking slightly as he relit the cigar that never left his mouth. He questioned her closely, all business. Zeitlin alone decided when their conversations would be warm and when they would be cold. Not for the first time, Lala pitied the children of people of quality who could not love like more middling people.

Then, taking a deep breath, she looked at her employer, at the intense gaze of this slim, handsome man with the fair moustache and Edward VII beard, and realized that if anyone could be trusted to bring her Sashenka home, the baron could.

'Please stop crying, Mrs Lewis,' said Baron Zeitlin, proprietor of the Anglo-Russian Naphtha-Oil Bank of Baku and St Petersburg, handing her a silk handkerchief from his frock coat. Calmness in moments of crisis was not just a requirement of life and a mark of civilization but an art, almost a religion. 'Crying won't get her out. Now sit down. Gather yourself.'

Zeitlin saw Lala take a breath, touch her hair and smooth down her dress. She sat, hands together, bracing herself, trying to be calm.

'Have you mentioned this to anyone else in the house?'

'No,' replied Lala, whose heart-shaped face seemed to Zeitlin unbearably appealing when decorated with her crystal tears. Only her high voice failed to fit the picture. 'But Pantameilion knows.'

Zeitlin walked back round his desk and pulled a velvet bellrope. The parlourmaid appeared, a light-footed peasant girl with the snub nose that marked her as a child of the family estates in Ukraine.

'Luda, ask Pantameilion to decarbonize the Pierce-Arrow in the garage,' said Zeitlin.

'Yes, master,' she said, bowing slightly from the waist: peasants from the real countryside still bowed to their masters, Zeitlin reflected, but nowadays those from the cities just sneered.

As Luda closed the study door, Zeitlin sank down in his high-backed chair, pulled out his green leather cigar box with the gold monogram and absent-mindedly drew out a cigar. Stroking the rolled leaves, he eased off the band and smelt it, drawing the length of it under his nose and against his moustache so that it touched his lips. Then with a flash of his chunky cufflinks, he took the silver cutter and snipped off the tip. Moving slowly and sensuously, he flipped the cigar between finger and thumb, spinning it round his hand like the baton of the leader of a marching band. Then he placed it in his mouth and raised the jewelled silver lighter in the shape of a rifle (a gift of the War Minister, for whom he manufactured the wooden stocks of rifles for Russian infantrymen). The smell of kerosene rose.

'*Calme-toi*, Mrs Lewis,' he told Lala. 'Everything's possible. Just a few phone calls and she'll be home.'

But beneath this show of confidence, Zeitlin's heart was palpitating: his only child, his Sashenka, was in a cell somewhere. The thought of a policeman or, worse, a criminal, even a murderer, touching her gave him a burning pain in his chest, compounded by shame, a whiff of embarrassment, and a sliver of guilt – but he soon dismissed that. The arrest was either a mistake or the fruit of intrigue by some jealous war contractor – but calm good sense, peerless connections and the generous application of geld would correct it. He had fixed greater challenges than releasing an innocent teenager: his rise from the provinces to his current status in St Petersburg, his place on the Table of Ranks, his blossoming fortune, even Sashenka's presence at the Smolny Institute, all these were testament to his steely calculation of the odds and meticulous preparation, easy luck, and uninhibited embrace of his rightful prizes.

'Mrs Lewis, do you know anything about the arrest?' he asked a little sheepishly. Powerful in so many ways, he was vulnerable in his own household. 'If you know something, anything that could help Sashenka . . .'

Lala's eyes met and held his through the grey smoke. 'Perhaps you should ask her uncle?'

'Mendel? But he's in exile, isn't he?'

'Quite possibly.'

He caught the edge in a voice that always sounded as if it was singing a lullaby to a child, his child, and recognized the glance that told him he hardly knew his own daughter.

'But before his last arrest,' she continued, 'he told me this house wasn't safe for him any more.'

'Not safe any more . . .' murmured Zeitlin. She meant that the secret police were watching his house. 'So Mendel has escaped from Siberia? And Sashenka's in contact with him? That bastard Mendel! Why doesn't anyone tell me anything?'

Mendel, his wife's brother, Sashenka's uncle, had recently been arrested and sentenced to five years of administrative exile for revolutionary conspiracy. But now he had escaped, and maybe somehow he had entangled Sashenka in his grubby machinations.

Lala stood up, shaking her head.

'Well, Baron, I know it's not my place . . .' She smoothed her floral dress, which served only to accentuate her curves. Zeitlin watched her, fiddling with a string of jade worry beads, the only un-Russian hint in the entire stalwartly Russian study.

There was a sudden movement behind them.

'*Shalom aleichem!*' boomed a broad-shouldered, bearded man in a sable greatcoat, astrakhan hat

24

and high boots like a hussar. 'Don't ask me about last night! I lost every kopek in my pocket – but who's counting?'

The door to the baron's sanctuary had been shoved open and Gideon Zeitlin's aura of cologne, vodka and animal sweat swept into the study. The baron winced, knowing that his brother tended to call on the house only when he needed his funds replenished.

'Last night's girl cost me a pretty fortune,' said Gideon. 'First the cards. Then dinner at the Donan. Cognac at the Europa. Gypsies at the Bear. But it was worth it. That's paradise on earth, eh? Apologies to you, Mrs Lewis!' He made a theatrical bow, big black eyes glinting beneath bushy black brows. 'But what else is there in life except fresh lips and skin? Tomorrow be damned! I feel marvellous!'

Gideon Zeitlin touched Mrs Lewis's neck, making her jump, as he sniffed her carefully pinned hair. 'Lovely!' he murmured as he strode round the desk to kiss his elder brother wetly, twice on the cheeks and once on the lips.

He tossed his wet fur coat into the corner, where it settled like a living animal, and arranged himself on the divan.

'Gideon, Sashenka's in trouble . . .' Zeitlin started wearily.

'I heard, Samoilo. Those ideeeots!' bellowed Gideon, who blamed all the mistakes of mankind on a conspiracy of imbeciles that included

25

everyone except himself. 'I was at the newspaper and I got a call from a source. I haven't slept from last night yet. But I'm glad Mama's not alive to see this one. Are you feeling OK, Samoilo? Your ticker? How's your indigestion? Lungs? Show me your tongue?'

'I'm bearing up,' replied Zeitlin. 'Let me see yours.'

Although the brothers were opposites in appearance and character, the younger impecunious journalist and the older fastidious nabob shared the very Jewish conviction that they were on the verge of death at all times from angina pectoris, weak lungs (with a tendency towards consumption), unstable digestion and stomach ulcers, exacerbated by neuralgia, constipation and haemorrhoids. St Petersburg's finest doctors competed with the specialists of Berlin, London and the resorts of Biarritz, Bad Ems and Carlsbad for the right to treat these invalids, whose bodies were living mines of gold for the medical profession.

'I'll die at any moment, probably making love to the general's girl again – but what the devil! Gehenna – Hell – the Book of Life and all that Jewish claptrap be damned! Everything in life is here and now. There's nothing after! The commander-in-chief and the general staff' – Gideon's long-suffering wife Vera and their two daughters – 'are cursing me. Me? Of all people! Well, I just can't resist it. I won't ask again for a long time, for years even! My gambling debts are . . .' He whispered into his brother's ear. 'Now hand over my bar mitzvah present, Samoilo: gimme the *mazuma* and I'm off on my quest!'

'Where to?' Zeitlin unlocked a wooden box on his desk, using a key that hung on his gold watch chain. He handed over two hundred roubles, quite a sum.

Zeitlin spoke Russian like a court chamberlain, without a Jewish accent, and he thought that Gideon scattered his speech with Yiddish and Hebrew phrases just to tease him about his rise, to remind him of whence they came. In his view, his younger brother still carried the smell of their father's courtyard in the Pale of Settlement, where the Jews of the Tsarist Empire had to live.

He watched as Gideon seized the cash and spread it into a fan. 'That's for me. Now I need the same again to grease the palms of some ideeeots.'

Zeitlin, who rarely refused Gideon's requests because he felt guilty about his brother's fecklessness, opened his little box again.

'I'll pick up some London fruitcake from the English Shop; find where Sashenka is; toss some of your vile *mazuma* to policemen and inkshitters and get her out if I can. Call the newspaper if you want me. Mrs Lewis!' Another insolent bow – and Gideon was gone, slamming the door behind him.

A second later, it opened again. 'You know Mendel's skulking around? He's out of the clink!

27

If I see that *schmendrik*, I'll punch him so hard his fortified boot will land in Lenin's lap. Those Bolsheviks are ideeeots!' The door slammed a second time.

Zeitlin raised his hands to his face for a few seconds, forgetting Lala was still there. Then, sighing deeply, he reached for the recently installed telephone, a leather box with a listening device hooked on to the side. He tapped it thrice on the top and spoke into the mouthpiece: 'Hello, exchange? Put me through to the Interior Minister, Protopopov! Petrograd 234. Yes, now please!'

Zeitlin relit his cigar as he waited for the exchange to connect him to the latest Interior Minister.

'The baroness is in the house?' he asked. Lala nodded. 'And the old people, the travelling circus?' This was his nickname for his parents-in-law, who lived over the garage. Lala nodded again. 'Leave the baroness to me. Thanks, Mrs Lewis.'

As Lala shut the door, he asked no one in particular: 'What on earth has Sashenka done?' and then his voice changed:

'Ah, hello, Minister, it's Zeitlin. Recovered from your poker losses, eh? I'm calling about a sensitive family matter. Remember my daughter? Yes, her. Well . . .'

CHAPTER 5

At the Gendarmerie's Temporary House of Detention within the red walls of the Kresty Prison, Sashenka was waiting, still in her sable coat and Arctic snowfox stole. Her Smolny dress and pinafore were already smeared with greasy fingermarks and black dust. She had been left in a holding area with concrete floors and chipped wooden walls.

A pathway had been worn smooth from the door to benches and thence to the counter, which had slight hollows where the prisoners had leaned their elbows as they were booked. Everything had been marked by the thousands who had passed through. Hookers, safebreakers, murderers, revolutionaries waited with Sashenka. She was fascinated by the women: the nearest, a bloated walrus of a woman with rough bronze-pink skin and an army coat covering what appeared to be a ballerina's tutu, stank of spirits.

'What do you want, you motherfucker?' she snarled. 'What are you staring at?' Sashenka, mortified, was suddenly afraid this monster would strike her. Instead the woman leaned over, horribly close. 'I'm an educated woman, not some street-walker like I seem. It was that bastard that did this to me, he beat me and . . .' Her name was called but she kept talking until the gendarme opened the counter and dragged her away. As the metal door slammed behind her, she was still shouting, 'You motherfuckers, I'm an educated woman, it was that bastard who broke me . . .'

Sashenka was relieved when the woman was gone, and then ashamed until she reminded herself that the old hooker was not a proletarian, merely a degenerate bourgeoise.

The corridors of the House of Detention were busy: men and women were being delivered to their cells, taken to interrogations, despatched on the long road to Siberian exile. Some sobbed, some slept; all of life was there. The gendarme behind the counter kept looking at her as if she was a peacock in a pigsty.

Sashenka took her poetry books out of her book bag. Pretending to read, she flicked through the pages. When she came across a piece of cigarette paper with tiny writing on it, she glanced around, smiled broadly at any policeman who happened to be looking at her, and then popped it in her mouth. Uncle Mendel had taught her what to do. The papers did not taste too bad and they were not too hard to swallow. By the time it was her turn to be booked at the counter, she had consumed all of the incriminating evidence. She asked for a glass of water.

'You've got to be joking,' replied the policeman, who had taken her name, age and nationality but refused to tell her anything about the charges she faced. 'This isn't the Europa Hotel, girl.'

She raised her grey eyes to him. 'Please,' she said.

He banged a chipped mug of water on to the counter, with a croaking laugh.

As she drank, a gendarme called her name. Another with a bunch of keys opened a reinforced steel door and she entered the next layer of the Kresty. Sashenka was ordered into a small room and made to strip, then she was searched by an elephantine female warder in a dirty white apron. No one except dear Lala had ever seen her naked (her governess still drew her a bath every evening) but she told herself it did not matter. Nothing mattered except her cause, her holy grail, and that she was here at last, where every decent person should be.

The woman returned her clothes but took her coat, stole and book bag. Sashenka signed for them and received a chit in return.

Then they photographed her. She waited in a line of women, who scratched themselves constantly. The stench was of sweat, urine, menstrual blood. The photographer, an old man in a brown suit and string tie, with no teeth and eyes like holes in a hollow pumpkin, manhandled her in front of a tripod bearing an enormous camera that looked

31

like a concertina. He disappeared under a cloth, his muffled voice calling out:

'OK, full face. Stand up. Look left, look right. A Smolny girl, eh, with a rich daddy? You won't be in here long. I was one of the first photographers in Piter. I do family portraits too if you want to mention me to your papa . . . There we are!'

Sashenka realized her arrest was now recorded for ever – and she gave a wide smile that encouraged the photographer's sales patter.

'A smile! What a turn-up! Most of the animals that come through here don't care what they look like – but you're going to look wonderful. That, I promise.'

Then a yellow-skinned warder not much older than Sashenka led her towards a holding cell. Just as she was about to enter, an official in a belted grey uniform emerged from nowhere. 'That'll do, boy. I'll take over.'

This popinjay with some stripes on his shoulderboards appeared to be in charge. Sashenka was disappointed: she wanted to be treated like the real thing, like a peasant or worker. Yet the Smolny girl in her was relieved as he took her arm gently. Around her, the cold stone echoed with shouts, grunts, the clink of keys, slamming of doors and turning of locks.

Someone was shouting, 'Fuck you, fuck the Tsar, you're all German spies!'

But the chief warder, in his tunic and boots, paid no attention. His hand was still on Sashenka's arm and he was chatting very fast. 'We've had a few students and schoolboys in – but you're the first from Smolny. Well, I love "politicals". Not criminals, they're scum. But "politicals", people of education, they make my job a pleasure. I might surprise you: I'm not your typical warder here. I read and I've even read a bit of your Marx and your Plekhanov. Truly. Two other things: I have a fondness for Swiss chocolates and Brocard's eau de cologne. My sense of smell is highly sophisticated: see my nose?' Sashenka looked dutifully as he flared narrow nostrils. 'I have the sensory buds of an aesthete yet here I am, stuck in this dive. You're something to do with Baron Zeitlin? Here we are! Make sure he knows my name is Volkov, Sergeant S. P. Volkov.'

'I will, Sergeant Volkov,' Sashenka replied, trying not to gag on the suffocating aroma of lavender cologne.

'I'm not your typical warder, am I? Do I surprise you?'

'Oh yes, Sergeant, you do.'

'That's what everyone says. Now, Mademoiselle Zeitlin, here is your berth. Don't forget, Sergeant Volkov is your special friend. Not your typical warder!'

'Not at all typical.'

'You'll miss my cologne in a minute,' he warned.

A guard opened a cell door and manhandled her inside. She turned to reach for the chief warder, even raising a hand, but he was gone. The smell of women crowded into a confined space blasted her nostrils. This is the real Russia! she told herself, feeling the rottenness creeping into her clothes.

The cell door slammed behind her. The locks turned. Sashenka stood, shoulders hunched, aware of the dark cramped space behind her seething with shadowy, vigilant life. Farting, grunting, sneezing, singing and coughing vied with whispers and the flick of cards being dealt.

Sashenka slowly turned, feeling the rancid breath of twenty or thirty women, hot then cool, hot then cool, on her face. A single kerosene lamp lightened the gloom. The prisoners lined the walls and lay on mattresses on the cold dirty floor, sleeping, playing cards, some even cuddling. Two half-naked crones were picking lice out of each other's pubic hair like monkeys. A low partition marked off the latrine, from whence came groans and liquid explosions.

'Hurry up!' shouted the next in line.

A plump woman with slanting oriental eyes lay reading Tolstoy's *Confessions*, while a cadaverous woman in a man's army greatcoat over a peasant smock declaimed from a pornographic pamphlet about the Empress, Rasputin and their mutual friend, Madame Vyrubova. '"Three is better than one," said the monk. "Anya Vyrubova, your tits are juicy as a Siberian seal – but nothing beats a wanton imperial cunt like yours, my Empress!"' There was laughter. The reader stopped.

'Who's this? Countess Vyrubova slumming it from court?' The creature in the greatcoat was on her feet. Stepping on a sleeping figure who howled in complaint, she rushed at Sashenka and seized her hair. 'You rich little bitch, don't look at me like that!'

Sashenka was afraid for the first time since her arrest, properly afraid, with fear that lurched in her guts and burned in her throat. Before she had time to think, she was punched in the mouth and fell, only to be crushed as the creature threw herself on top of her. She struggled to breathe. Fearing she was going to die, she thought of Lala, Grand-maman at school, her pony in the country . . . But suddenly the attacker was lifted right off her and tossed sideways.

'Careful, bitch. Don't touch her! I think this one's ours.' The plump woman holding an open copy of Tolstoy stood over her. 'Sashenka? The cell elders welcome you. You'll meet the committee in the morning. Let's get some sleep. You can share my mattress. I'm Comrade Natasha. You don't know me, but I know exactly who you are.'

CHAPTER 6

Captain Sagan of the Gendarmerie dropped into his favourite chair at the Imperial Yacht Club on Greater Maritime Street and was just rubbing a toke of cocaine into his gums when his adjutant appeared in the doorway.

'Your Excellency, may I report?'

Sagan saw the blotchy-skinned adjutant glance quickly around the enormous, empty room with its leather chairs and newspapers in English, French and Russian. Beyond the billiard table hung portraits of bemedalled club chairmen, and at the far end of the room, above a blazing fire of apple-scented wood, the watery blue eyes of the Emperor Nicholas II. 'Go ahead, Ivanov.'

'Your Excellency, we've arrested the terrorist revolutionaries. Found dynamite, chargers, Mauser pistols, leaflets. There's a schoolgirl among them. The general says he wants you to start on her right away before her bigshot papa gets her out. I've a phaeton waiting outside.'

Captain Sagan got to his feet and sighed. 'Fancy a drink, Ivanov, or a pinch of this?' He held out the silver box. 'Dr Gemp's new tonic for fatigue and headaches.'

'The general said you should hurry.'

'I'm tired,' Sagan said, although his heart was racing. It was the third winter of the war, and he was overworked to the point of exhaustion. Not only was he a gendarme, he was also a senior officer in the Okhrana, the Tsar's secret police. 'German spies, Bolsheviks, Social Revolutionaries, every sort of traitor. We can't hang them fast enough. And then there's Rasputin. At least sit for a moment.'

'All right. Cognac,' Ivanov said, a shade too reluctantly for Sagan's liking.

'Cognac? Your tastes are becoming rather expensive, Ivanov.' Sagan tinkled a silver bell. A waiter, as long and thin as a flute, glided drunkenly through the door, as if on skis. 'Two cognacs and make it quick,' Sagan ordered, savouring the aroma of cigars, cologne and shoe polish, the essence of officers' messes and gentlemen's clubs across the Empire. When the glasses arrived, the two men stood up, toasted the Tsar, downed their brandies and hurried into the lobby.

They pulled on their uniform greatcoats and *shapkas* and stepped out into a numbing cold. Disorderly, shapeless snowflakes danced around them. It was already midnight but a full moon made the fresh snow glow an eerie blue. Cocaine, Sagan decided, was the secret policeman's ideal tonic in that it intensified his scrutiny, sharpening his vision. There stood his phaeton, a taxi-carriage with one horse snorting geysers of breath, its driver a snoring bundle of clothing. Ivanov gave him a shove and the driver's bald head appeared out of his sheepskin, pink, shiny and bleary-eyed, like a grotesque baby born blind drunk.

Sagan, heart still palpitating, scanned the street. To the left, the golden dome of St Isaac's Cathedral loomed ominously over the houses as if about to crush them. Down to the right, he could see the doorway of the Zeitlin residence. He checked his surveillance team. Yes, a moustachioed figure in a green coat and bowler hat lurked near the corner: that was Batko, ex-NCO Cossack, smoking a cigarette in the doorway of the apartments opposite. (Cossacks and ex-NCOs made the best 'external agents', those who worked on surveillance.) And there was a sleeping droshky driver a little further down the street: Sagan hoped he was not really asleep.

A Rolls-Royce, with chains on its wheels and a Romanov crest on its doors, skidded past. Sagan knew that it belonged to Grand Duke Sergei, who would be going home with the ballerina mistress he shared with his cousin Grand Duke Andrei.

From the Blue Bridge over the Moika came the echo of shouts, the thud of punches and the crunch of boots and bodies on compacted snow. Some sailors from the Kronstadt base were fighting soldiers – dark blue versus khaki.

Then, just as Sagan had one foot on the

phaeton's step, a Benz limousine rumbled up. Its uniformed driver leaped out and opened the leather-lined door. Out of it stepped an overripe, ruddy-cheeked figure in a fur coat. Manuilov-Manesevich, spy, war profiteer, friend of Rasputin, born a Jew, converted to Orthodoxy, pushed past Sagan and hurried into the Imperial Yacht Club. Inside the limousine, Sagan glimpsed crushed scarlet satin and mink on a pale throat. A waft of sweat and cigar smoke disgusted him. He got into the carriage.

'This is what the Empire has come to,' he told Ivanov. 'Yid spies and influence-peddlers. A scandal every day!'

'Yaaaa!' the driver yelled, cracking his whip a little too close to Sagan's nose. The phaeton lurched forward.

Sagan leaned back and let the lights of Peter the Great's city flow past him. The brandy was a bullet of molten gold scouring his belly. Here was his life, in the capital of the world's greatest empire, ruled by its stupidest people in the midst of the most terrible war the world had ever known. Sagan told himself that the Emperor was lucky that he and his colleagues still believed in him and his right to rule; lucky they were so vigilant; lucky that they would stop at nothing to save this fool Tsar and his hysterical wife, whoever her friends were . . .

'Y'wanna know what I think, *barin?*' said the driver, sitting sideways to his passengers, his warthog nose illuminated by the phaeton's swinging lantern. 'Oats is going up again! One more price hike and we won't be able to feed our horses. There was a time, I remember it well, when oats was only . . .'

Oats, oats, oats, that was all Sagan heard from the damn drivers of carriages and sleighs. He breathed deeply as the cocaine-charged blood gushed through his temples like a mountain stream.

CHAPTER 7

'Where are you going tonight?' Zeitlin asked his wife.

'I don't know,' sighed Ariadna Zeitlin dreamily. She was reclining on the divan in her flesh-coloured boudoir, dressed only in stockings and a slip. She closed her eyes as her lady's maid primped her hair with curling tongs. Her voice was low and husky, the words running together as if she was already a little high. 'Want to come along for the ride?'

'It's important, my dear.' He took a chair close to the divan.

'Well, maybe Baroness Rozen's for cocktails, then a dinner at the Donan, some dancing at the Aquarium – I love that place, have you seen the beautiful fish all around the walls? – and then, well, I'm not sure . . . Ah Nyana, let's see, I fancy something with brocade for tonight.'

Two maids came out of her dressing room, Nyana holding a jewellery box, the other girl with a heap of dresses over her arm.

'Come on, Ariadna. I need to know where you're going,' snapped Zeitlin.

Ariadna sat up sharply. 'What is it? You look quite upset. Has the Bourse crashed or . . .' and here she gave him a tender smile, flashing her white teeth, 'or are you learning how to be jealous? It's never too late, you know. A girl likes to be cherished.'

Zeitlin inhaled his cigar. Their marriage had diminished to these brief exchanges before each plunged, separately, into the St Petersburg night, though they still attended balls and formal dinners together. He glanced at the unmade bed, where his wife spent so much time sleeping during the day. He looked at the dresses in batiste, chiffon and silk, at the bottles of potions and scents, at the half-smoked cigarettes, at the healing crystals, and all those other fads and luxuries; but he looked longest at Ariadna with her snow-white skin, her wide shoulders and her violet eyes. She was still beautiful, even if her eyes were bloodshot and the veins stood out in her temples.

She opened her hands and reached out to him, her tuberose scent mixing deliciously with that of her skin, but he was too anxious to play their usual games.

'Sashenka's been arrested by the gendarmes,' he told her. 'Right at the school gates. She's in the Kresty for the night. Can you imagine the cells there?'

Ariadna blinked. A tiny frown appeared on her pale face. 'It must be a misunderstanding. She's so bookish, it's hard to imagine she'd do anything silly.' She looked at him. 'Surely you can get her out tonight, Samuil? Call the Interior Minister. Doesn't he owe you money?'

'I've just called Protopopov and he says it's serious.'

'Nyana?' Ariadna beckoned to her lady's maid. 'I think I'll wear the mauve brocade with the gold leaf and flounces from Madame Chanceau, and I'll have the pearl choker and the sapphire brooch . . .'

Zeitlin was losing his patience. 'That's enough, Ariadna.' He switched to Yiddish so the servants could not understand. 'Stop lolling there like a chorus girl, dammit! We're talking about Sashenka.' He switched back to Russian, casting a black glance around the disorderly room: 'Girls! Leave us alone!' Zeitlin knew that his tempers were as rare as they were fearsome and the three maids abandoned the dresses and jewels and curling tongs and scurried out.

'Was that really necessary?' asked Ariadna, her voice quivering, tears welling in her kohl-smeared eyes.

But Zeitlin was all business. 'Are you seeing Rasputin?'

'Yes, I'm visiting the Elder Grigory tonight. After midnight. Don't speak of him in that mocking tone, Samuil. When Dr Badaev's Mongolian lama hypnotized me at the House of Spirits, he said I needed a special teacher. He was right. The Elder Grigory helps me, nourishes me spiritually. He says I'm a gentle lamb in a metal world, and that you crush me. You think I'm happy in this house?'

'We're here to talk about Sashenka,' he protested, but Ariadna's voice was rising.

'Remember, Samuil, when we used to go to the ballet, every set of binoculars was aimed at *me*, not the stage? "What is Baroness Zeitlin wearing? Look at her eyes, her jewels, her lovely shoulders . . ." When the officers looked at me, they thought, there's a fine racehorse, a thoroughbred – it might be worth having a guilty conscience for that one! Weren't you proud of me then, Samuil? And now – just look at me!'

Zeitlin stood up angrily. 'This is not about you, Ariadna. Try to remember we're talking about our child!'

'I'm sorry. I'm listening . . .'

'Mendel's back from exile.' He saw her shrug. 'Oh, so you knew that? Well, he's probably played some part in our daughter's incarceration.'

He knelt down beside the divan and took her hands. 'Look, Protopopov doesn't control things. Even Premier Sturmer has no influence – he's about to be replaced. Everything's in the hands of the Empress and Rasputin. So this time I *want* you to go to Rasputin's – I need you to go there! I'm delighted you have access, and I don't care how long you spend being pawed by the sacred peasant. Tell him he's in luck tonight. Only *you* can do this, Ariadna. Just get in there and petition all of them – Rasputin, the Empress's friends, whoever, to get Sashenka out!'

'You're sending me on a mission?' Ariadna shook herself like a cat flicking off rain.

'Yes.'

'Me on a political mission? I like the sound of that.' She paused and Zeitlin could almost hear the wheels turning as she came to a decision. 'I'll show you what a good mama I am.' She rose from the divan and pulled the braid cord by her side. 'Girls – get back in here! I've got to look my best.' The maids returned, looking gingerly at Zeitlin. 'And what will you be doing, Samuil?'

'I'm going to hold my nose and go to Prince Andronnikov's. They'll all be there.'

Ariadna seized Zeitlin's face between her hands. Her spicy breath and tuberose scent made his eyes water.

'You and me on a mission, Samuil!'

Despite the coarseness of her skin – the mark of drink and opium – her face, he thought, was still magnificent; the bruised lips, the overbite and long upper lip utterly, selfishly greedy; her shoulders and legs still superb despite the protuberant belly. Whatever her flaws, Ariadna had the look of a woman to whom rough pleasure came almost too easily, as easily as bruises to a ripe peach. Now, with the kohl on her eyes smeared with tears, she looked like a drugged Cleopatra. 'Samuil, can I take the Russo-Balt?'

'Done,' said Zeitlin, happy for her to use the limousine. He stood up and kissed her.

Ariadna gave a little shiver of pleasure, opened

the top of her diamond and gold clock, took an Egyptian cigarette out of the hidden compartment, and looked up at him with eyes that held the echo of empty rooms.

Thinking how she had become like a lost child and blaming himself, he lit her cigarette and then the cold cigar he was holding.

'I'll be off then,' he said, watching her inhale and then open her lips to let the blue smoke dance its way out.

'Good luck, Samuil,' she called after him.

He did not want to be late for Prince Andronnikov – Sashenka's welfare depended on him – yet he stopped and glanced back before he closed the door.

'How does this look? And this? Look, it moves as I walk. See, Luda?' Ariadna was laughing as the maids bustled around her. 'Don't you agree, Nyuna, Monsieur Worth's dresses put the rest to shame! I can't wait for them to see this at the Aquarium . . .'

With a sinking heart, Zeitlin realized that the moment his wife left the house she would forget all about him and Sashenka.

CHAPTER 8

Throughout the night, Sashenka clung to Natasha's whale-like bulk.

The older woman snored and when she turned over she pushed Sashenka, who was almost too afraid to move, off the mattress. Sashenka lay there, her hips ground into the freezing stone floor, but grateful just to be next to Natasha, safe. Her mouth felt as if it was ballooning where she had been hit, and her hands were shaking. She was still afraid the monster would hit her again – or maybe she would come and stab her in a frenzy during the night? They would all have knives. Sashenka peered through the semidarkness at the tangle of female bodies – one half-naked with bare shrivelled breasts and long nipples like bottle-stoppers – sensing the heat and rot rising around her. She prayed someone would come soon to rescue her.

Lanterns flickered outside the cell, as a warder double-locked the doors. A cleaner mopped the corridors. The smell of naphtha and disinfectant temporarily defeated that of piss and shit, but not for long. Sashenka hoped every grunt and creak and slam signalled her deliverance, but no one came. The interminable night stretched out before her, cold, frightening, hostile.

'We got a message on the cell telegraph that you were coming,' Natasha had whispered to Sashenka. 'We're almost family, you and I. I'm your uncle Mendel's wife. We met in exile. I bet you didn't know he married a Yakut? Yes, a real Siberian. Oh, I see – you didn't know he was married at all. Well, that's Mendel for you, the born conspirator. I didn't even know he had a niece until today. Anyway, he trusts you. Keep your wits about you: there are always opportunities . . .'

Now Natasha grunted and heaved in her sleep, saying something in her native language. Sashenka remembered that Yakuts believed in shamans and spirits. A woman shouted, 'I'll cut your throat!' Another whimpered, 'Lost . . . lost . . . lost.' There was a brawl in the men's cell next door; someone was wounded, and warders dragged him away groaning and brought a mop to clean up. Doors opened and slammed. Sashenka listened to consumptive coughing and squelching bowels, the footsteps of the warders, and the bubbling of Natasha's stomach. She could not quite believe this was happening to her. Even though Sashenka was proud to be there, the fear, the stink and the endless night were making her desperate. Yet hadn't Uncle Mendel told her prison was a rite of passage? And what had Natasha the Yakut whispered before she fell asleep? Yes: 'Mendel trusts you!'

It was because of Mendel that she was here, because of their meeting the previous summer. The family's summers were spent at Zemblishino, an estate south of the city near the Warsaw Highway. Jews were not allowed to live in the capital or own property unless they were merchant princes like Baron Zeitlin. Sashenka's father owned not only the mansion in town but also the manor house with white pillars, the woodlands and the park. Sashenka knew that her father was not the only Jewish magnate in St Petersburg. Another Jewish baron, Poliakoff, the railway king, lived in Prince Menshikov's old red-brick palace, the first house built in Peter the Great's new city, on the new quay almost opposite the Winter Palace.

Each summer Sashenka and Lala were left to their own devices in the country, though sometimes Zeitlin persuaded them to play tennis or go bicycling. Her mother, usually in the frenzy of a neuralgic crisis, mystical fad or broken heart, rarely left her room – and would soon rush back to the city. Lala spent her days collecting mushrooms and blueberries or riding Almaz the chestnut pony. Sashenka read on her own; she was always happy on her own.

That summer, Uncle Mendel had been staying too. A tiny twisted man with thick pince-nez on a big bent nose and a club foot, he worked all night in the library, smoking self-rolled *makhorka* cigarettes and brewing Turkish coffee that filled the house with its scalded, nutty aroma. He slept above the stables, lying in all morning, rising only after lunch. He seemed incapable of adapting to the summer, always wearing the same filthy dark suit and a crumpled shirt with a grimy collar. His shoes always had holes in them. Alongside her dapper father and fashionable mother, he really was a stranger from another planet. If he caught Sashenka's eye, he scowled and glanced away. He looked terribly ill, she thought, with his pale blotchy skin and asthmatic wheeze, the fruit of years in prison and exile in Siberia.

The family despised Mendel. Even Sashenka's mother, Mendel's own sister, disliked him – but she let him stay. 'He's all on his own, poor sad creature,' she would say disdainfully.

And then one night Sashenka could not sleep. It was 3am. The summer was hot and the heat gathered in her room under the roof. She wanted some lemon juice so she came downstairs, past the portrait of Count Orlov-Chesmensky, a former owner of the manor, the fifteen crystal peacocks on the shelf, and the English grandfather clock, and into the deliciously cool hall with its black and white flagstone floor. She saw the library lights were still on and smelt the coffee and smoke blending in the warm, rosy night.

Mendel opened the library door and Sashenka stepped aside into the cloakroom, from where she watched her uncle limp out with a gleam in his bloodshot eyes, a sheaf of valuable papers gripped in his claw-like hands.

The trapped miasma of an entire night's chainsmoking poured out like a ghostly tidal wave. Sashenka waited until he had gone and then darted into the library to look at the books that so gripped him that he was happy to go to prison for them. The table was empty.

'Curious, Sashenka?' It was Mendel at the door, his voice incongruously deep and rich, his clothes defiantly moth-eaten.

She jumped. 'I was just interested,' she said.

'In my books?'

'Yes.'

'I hide them when I've finished. I don't like people knowing my business or even my thoughts.' He hesitated. 'But you're a serious person. The only intellectual in this family.'

'How do you know that, Uncle, since you've never bothered to speak to me?' Sashenka was delighted and surprised.

'The others are just capitalist decadents and our family rabbi belongs in the Middle Ages. I judge you by what you read. Mayakovsky. Nekrasov. Blok. Jack London.'

'So you've been watching me?'

Mendel's pince-nez were so greasy the lenses were barely transparent. He limped over to the English collection, the full set of Dickens bound in kid with the gold Zeitlin crest, and pulling out

51

one, he reached behind and handed her a well-thumbed old book: *What Is to Be Done?* by Chernyshevsky.

'Read it now. When you finish, you'll find the next book here behind *David Copperfield*. Understood? We'll take it from there.'

'Take what? From where?'

But Mendel was gone and she was alone in the library.

That was how it started. The next night, she could hardly wait until everyone was asleep before she crept down, savouring the smells of coffee and acrid *makhorka* tobacco as she drew closer to the set of Dickens.

'Ready for the next? Your analysis of the book?' Mendel had said without looking up.

'Rakhmetov is the most compelling hero I have ever known,' she told him, returning his book. 'He is selfless, dedicated. Nothing stands in the way of his cause. The "special man" touched by history. I want to be like him.'

'We all do,' he replied. 'I know many Rakhmetovs. It was the first book I read too. And not just me but Lenin as well.'

'Tell me about Lenin. And what is a Bolshevik? Are you Bolshevik, Menshevik, Social Revolutionary, Anarchist?'

Mendel observed her as if she was a zoological specimen, narrowing his eyes, inhaling the badly rolled *makhorka* that caught in his throat. He coughed productively.

'What's it to you? What do you think of Russia today, the workers, the peasants, the war?'

'I don't know. It seems as if . . .' She stopped, aware of his scathing stare.

'Go on. Speak up.'

'It's all wrong. It's so unjust. The workers are like slaves. We're losing the war. Everything's rotten. Am I a revolutionary? A Bolshevik?'

Mendel rolled a new cigarette, not hurriedly and with surprising delicacy, licked the paper and lit it. An orange flame flared up and died down.

'You don't know enough to be anything yet,' he told her. 'We must take our time. You are now the sole student on my summer course. Here's the next book.' He gave her Victor Hugo's novel of the French Revolution, *1793*.

The next night she was even more excited.

'Ready for more? Your analysis?'

'*Cimourdain had never been seen to weep,*' she quoted Hugo's description of his hero. '*He had an inaccessible and frigid virtue. A just but awful man. There are no half-measures for a revolutionary priest who must be infamous and sublime. Cimourdain was sublime, rugged, inhospitably repellent, gloomy but above all pure.*'

'Good. If Cimourdain was alive today, he'd be a Bolshevik. You have the sentiment; now you need the science. Marxism is a science. Now read this.' He held up a novel called *Lady Cynthia de Fortescue and the Love of the Cruel Colonel*. On its cover stood a lady with vermilion lipstick and cheeks like a puff adder, while a devilishly handsome officer with waxed moustaches and narrowed eyes lurked behind.

'What's this?' she asked.

'Just read what I give you.' Mendel was back at his desk, scratching with his pen.

In her bedroom, when she opened the book, she found Marx's *Communist Manifesto* hidden inside. This was soon followed by Plekhanov, Engels, Lassalle, more Marx, Lenin.

No one had ever spoken to Sashenka like Mendel. Her mother wanted her to be a foolish child preparing for a life of overheated balls, unhappy marriages and seedy adulteries. She adored her father but he barely noticed his 'little fox', regarding her as no more than a fluffy mascot. And darling Lala had long since submitted to her place in life, reading only novels like *Lady Cynthia de Fortescue and the Love of the Cruel Colonel*. As for Uncle Gideon, he was a degenerate sensualist who had tried to flirt with her, and once even patted her behind.

At meals and parties she barely spoke, so rapt was she by her short course in Marxism, so keen was she to ask Mendel more questions. Her mind was with him in his smoky library, far from her mother and father. Lala, who sometimes found her asleep with the lamp shining and some vulgar novel beside her, worried that she was reading too late. It was Mendel who exposed Sashenka to the grotesque injustice of capitalist society, to the oppression of workers and peasants, and showed her how Zeitlin – yes, her own father – was an exploiter of the working man.

But there was a solution, she learned: a class struggle that would progress through set stages to a workers' paradise of equality and decency. The Marxist theory was universal and utopian and all human existence fitted into its beautiful symmetry of history and justice. She could not understand why the workers of the industrial world, especially in St Petersburg and Moscow, the peasants in the villages of Russia and Ukraine, the footmen and maids in her father's houses, did not rise up and slay their masters at once. She had fallen in love with the ideas of dialectical materialism and the dictatorship of the proletariat.

Mendel treated Sashenka as an adult; more than a woman, as an adult *man*, a co-conspirator in the worthiest, most exclusive secret movement in the world. Before long they were meeting almost like lovers, in the twilight, at dawn and in the glowing night, in the stables, in the birch woods and blackberry thickets, on expeditions to collect mushrooms, even whispering by night in the dining hall, sealed within its yellow silk walls that were fragrant with carnations and lilac.

Yes, Sashenka thought now, the road to this stinking prison in the black St Petersburg winter had started on her father's fairytale estate on those summer nights when nightingales sang and the dusk was a hazy pink. But was she really such a threat to the throne of the Emperor that she should be arrested at the gates of the Smolny and tossed into this hell?

A woman behind Sashenka got up and staggered towards the slop bucket. Somehow she tripped over Sashenka and fell, cursing her. This time Sashenka grabbed the woman's soft throat, ready to fight, but the woman apologized and Sashenka found she suddenly didn't mind. Now she was tasting the real misery of Russia. Now she could tell them she did not just know big houses and limousines. Now she was a woman, a responsible adult, independent of her family. She tried to sleep but she could not.

In the sewers of the Empire, she felt alive for the first time.

CHAPTER 9

For his foray into the St Petersburg night, Zeitlin dressed in a new stiff collar and frock coat to which he attached his star of the Order of St Vladimir, second class, an honour enjoyed by only a very few Jewish industrialists.

At the bottom of the stairs, pausing for a moment with a hand against the exquisite turquoise tiles of the Dutch stove in the hall, he decided he had better tell his parents-in-law about Sashenka. He knew his wife would not bother. He passed through the empty drawing room and dining room, walled in canary and damask silk, then opened the baize door that led to the so-called Black Way, the dark underbelly of the house. The smell was quite different here, where the air was thick with butter, fat, boiling cabbage and sweat. It gave, thought Zeitlin, a hint of the other, older Russia.

Downstairs lived the cook and the chauffeur, but that was not where he was headed. Instead, Zeitlin started to climb the Black Way. Halfway up he leaned on a doorpost, exhausted and dizzy. Was it his heart, his indigestion, a touch of neurasthenia? Am I about to drop dead? he asked himself. Gideon was right, he had better call Dr Gemp again.

A hand touched his shoulder and he jumped. It was his old nanny, Shifra, a bone-white spectre in an orange housecoat and fluffy slippers who had cared for Sashenka before Lala's arrival.

'Would you approve the menu today?' she croaked. The household kept up the pretence that old Shifra was still in charge though Delphine now ran the kitchens. Shifra had been retired in tactful stages, without anyone telling her. 'I've consulted the powers, dear boy,' she added softly. 'I've glanced into the Book of Life. She'll be all right. Would you like a hot cocoa, Samoilo? Like the old days?'

Zeitlin nodded at the menu that Delphine had already shown him but refused the cocoa. The old woman floated away like a cobweb on the wind, as silently as she had emerged.

Alone again, he found to his surprise that there were tears in his eyes: it was that sensuous pull of childhood starting in the belly. His house felt suddenly alien to him, too big, too full of strangers. Where was his darling Sashenka? In a blinding flash of panic, he knew that his child was all that mattered.

But then the thousand threads of worldliness and wealth weaved around him again. How could he, Zeitlin, fail to fix anything? No one would dare to treat the girl roughly: surely everyone knew his connection to Their Imperial Majesties? His lawyer

58

Flek was on his way; the Interior Minister was calling the Director of Police, who was calling the Commander of the Separate Corps of Gendarmes, who in turn would be calling the chief of the Okhrana Security Section. He could not bear to think of Sashenka spending the night in a police station, let alone a prison cell. But what had she done? She seemed so demure, so correct, almost too serious for her age.

Parlourmaids and footmen lived further up the Black Way but he stopped on the second floor and opened the metal-lined door that led to the apartment over the garage. Here the smells became more foreign, and yet familiar to Samuil: chicken fat, gefilte fish, frying *babke* potatoes and the bite of *vishniak*. Noticing the *mezuzah* newly nailed to the doorpost, Zeitlin opened the door into what he called 'the travelling circus'.

In a large room, filled with precarious piles of books, candelabra, canvas cases and half-opened boxes, a tall old man with a white beard and ringlets, wearing a black kaftan and yarmulke, stood erect at a stand facing east towards Jerusalem, reciting the Eighteen Benedictions. A silver pointer with an outstretched finger showed his place in the open Talmud. The book was draped with silk, for the holy word could not be left uncovered. This man, Rabbi Abram Barmakid, was not Zeitlin's father but he was another link to the world of his childhood: this, Zeitlin thought wistfully, is where I came from.

Rabbi Barmakid, once the famous sage of Turbin with his own court and disciples, was now surrounded by sad vestiges of the silver paraphernalia that had previously beautified his prayerhouse and studyhouses. There stood the Ark with its scrolls in velvet covers and silver chains: golden lions with red-beaded eyes and blue-stoned manes kept watch. It was said the rabbi could work miracles. His lips moved quickly, his face seizing the joy and beauty of holy words in a time of disorder and downfall. He had just celebrated Yom Kippur and the Days of Awe camping in this godless house, and the only happy man in it was the one who had lost everything but kept his faith.

In 1915, the Grand Duke Nikolai Nikolaievich, the Commander-in-Chief, had declared all Jews potential German spies and driven them out of their villages. They were given a few hours to load centuries of life on to carts. Zeitlin had rescued the rabbi and his wife, putting them up in St Petersburg illegally because they had no permits. But while they denounced their godless daughter Ariadna, they were still proud, in spite of themselves, that she had married Zeitlin, a man with oilfields in Baku, ships in Odessa, forests in Ukraine . . .

'Is that you, Samuil?' a hoarse voice called out to him. In the cupboard-sized kitchen next door he found the rabbi's wife, Miriam, bewigged and wearing a silk housecoat, stirring a cauldron of soup at an old gas stove with two sideboards, the separation of milk from meat roughly enforced on a sprawl of half-washed kitchenware.

'Sashenka's been arrested,' said Samuil.

'Woe is me!' cried Miriam in her deep voice. 'Before the light, a deeper darkness! This is our punishment, our own Gehenna on earth, for children who all turned away from God, apostates each one. We died long ago and thanks to God, you can only die once. My son Mendel's a godless anarchist; Ariadna's lost to God: a daughter who, God protect her, goes out half-naked every night! My youngest boy, Avigdor, whose very name is dead to me, abandoned us altogether, long ago – where is he, still in London? And now our darling Silberkind's in trouble too.' In her childhood Sashenka had been blonde, and her grandparents still called her the Silberkind – the silver child. 'Well, we mustn't waste time.' The old woman started to pour honey into an empty plate.

'What are you cooking?'

'Honeycakes and chicken soup for Sashenka. In prison.'

They already knew, via the household grapevine. Zeitlin almost wept – while he called ministers, the old rabbi's wife was cooking honeycakes for her grandchild. He could hardly believe that these were the parents of Ariadna. How had they produced that hothouse flower in their Yiddish courtyard?

He stood watching Miriam as he had once watched his own mother in their family kitchen in a wooden-hutted village in the Pale of Settlement.

'I don't even know what she's been arrested for,' Zeitlin whispered.

Zeitlin was proud that he had never actually converted to Orthodoxy. He had not needed to do so. As a Merchant of the First Guild, he had the right to stay in St Petersburg even as a Jew – and just before the war he had been elevated to the rank of the Emperor's Secret Councillor, the equivalent of a lieutenant-general on the Table of Ranks. But despite all this, he was still a Jew, a discreet Jew but a Jew nonetheless. He still remembered the tune of Kol Nidre – and the excitement of asking the Four Questions at Passover.

'You're as white as a sheet, Samuil,' Miriam told him. 'Sit! Here, drink this!' She handed him a glass of *vishniak* and he downed it in one. Shaking his head slightly, he raised the empty glass to his mother-in-law and then, wordlessly kissing her blue-veined hand, he hurried downstairs, taking his beaver-skin coat and hat from Pantameilion at the front door. He was ready to begin.

CHAPTER 10

The surface of the frozen canal shone grittily in the moonlight as Captain Sagan's sleigh drew up outside the headquarters of the Department of Police, 16 Fontanka.

Taking the lift to the top floor, Sagan passed the two checkpoints, each with two gendarmes on duty, to enter the heart of the Empire's secret war against terrorists and traitors: the Tsar's Security Department, the Okhrana. Even late at night, the cream of the security service was at work up here – young clerks in pince-nez and blue uniforms sorting the card indexes (blue for Bolsheviks, red for Socialist Revolutionaries) and adding names to labyrinthine charts of revolutionary sects and cells.

Sagan was one of the organization's rising stars. He could have drawn the Bolshevik chart, with Lenin at its centre, in his sleep, even with its latest names and arrows. He hesitated before the chart for a moment just to relish his success. Here it was: all the Central Committee arrested, except Lenin and Zinoviev, plus six Duma members – the whole lot in Siberian exile, too broken ever to launch a revolution. Similarly, the Mensheviks: castrated as a group. The SR Battle Organization: broken. There were only a few more Bolshevik cells left to smash.

In the offices further along the corridor, the code-breakers with their greasy hair and flaky skin were poring over columns of hieroglyphics, and old-fashioned provincial officers in boots and whiskers leaned over maps of the Vyborg Side, planning raids. The security service needed all sorts, Sagan told himself, spotting a colleague who had been a revolutionary but had recently changed sides. Across the room he noticed the ex-burglar who was now the Okhrana's specialist house-breaker, and he greeted the homosexual Italian aristocrat, really a Jewish milkman's son from Mariupol, who specialized in sensitive interrogations . . . As for me, Sagan thought, I have my speciality too: turning revolutionaries into double agents. I could turn the Pope against God.

He ordered a clerk to bring the files on that night's raids and the reports of his *fileri* agents on the movements of the Jew Mendel Barmakid, and his niece, the Zeitlin girl.

CHAPTER 11

The scent of rosewater and perfumed candles at Prince Andronnikov's salon was so powerful that Zeitlin's head spun and his chest ached. He took a glass of champagne and downed it in one: he needed courage. He started to search the crowd, but knew that he mustn't seem too desperate. Does everyone know why I am here? Has the news about Sashenka spread? he asked himself. He hoped not.

The room was crowded with petitioners in winged collars, frock coats and medals, florid men of business puffing on cigars, but they were outnumbered by the bare shoulders of women, and shiny-cheeked, rose-lipped youths wearing velvet and rouge, smoking scented Egyptians through golden holders.

He was pulled aside by the obese ex-minister Khvostov, who began: 'It's only a matter of time now until the Emperor appoints a representative ministry – this can't go on, can it, Samuil?'

'Why not? It's gone on for three hundred years. It may not be perfect but the system is stronger than we think.' In Zeitlin's lifetime, however much the cards were shuffled, they had always ended in a configuration not entirely disadvantageous to his interests. It was his future, his luck sealed in the Book of Life. Things would go well – for him and for Sashenka, he reassured himself.

'Have you heard anything?' persisted Khvostov, gripping Zeitlin's arm. 'Who's he going to summon? We can't go on like this, can we, Samuil? I know you agree.'

Zeitlin tugged his arm free. 'Where is Andronnikov?'

'Right at the back . . . you'll never get there! It's too crowded. And another thing . . .' Zeitlin fled into the crowd. The heat and the perfumes were unbearable. Wet with sweat, the men's hands slipped and skidded on the soft, pale backs of the ladies. The cigar smoke was so dense that an acrid mist had formed, half feral, half exquisite. The Governor-General, old Prince Obolensky, real high nobility, and a couple of Golitsyns were there: knee-deep in the shit, thought Zeitlin. A pretty girl, who was kept in profitable three-way concubinage by the Deputy Interior Minister, the new War Minister and Grand Duke Sergei, was kissing Simnavich, Rasputin's secretary, with an open mouth, in front of everyone. Zeitlin took no satisfaction in this: he just thought of the rabbi and Miriam, back at home. They would not have believed that the court of the Russian Empire had somehow come to this.

In a clear tunnel through the tangled limbs and

necks of the crowd, Zeitlin saw a tiny bulging eye with such dense eyelashes that they were almost glued together. He was sure that the other eye and the rest of the body belonged to Manuilov-Manesevich, the dangerous huckster, police snitch, and now, disgracefully, the chief of staff of Premier Sturmer himself.

Zeitlin elbowed his way through but little Manuilov-Manesevich was always ahead of him and he never caught up. Instead he found himself at the doorway of Prince Andronnikov's holy of holies, newly redecorated like a Turkish harem – all swirling silks, with a fountain bursting out of a gold tap that formed the penis of a gilded boy Pan and, even more out of place, a large gold Buddha. A crystal chandelier with hundreds of candles dripping their wax only intensified the heat.

I probably paid for some of this tat, Zeitlin thought as he entered the tiny room packed with petitioners jostling for position. There, puffing on a hubble-bubble pipe and kissing the rosy neck of a boy in a page's uniform, was Andronnikov himself, with the Interior Minister perched next to him. Zeitlin had never abased himself before anyone: it was one of the many advantages of being rich. But there was no time for pride now.

'Hey, you spilt my drink! Where's your manners?' cried one petitioner.

'In a hurry to get somewhere, Baron Zeitlin?' sneered another. But Zeitlin, thinking only of his daughter, pushed through.

He found himself squatting next to Andronnikov and the minister.

'Ah, Zeitlin, sweetheart!' said Prince Andronnikov, who was wearing full face make-up and resembled a plump Chinese eunuch. 'Kisskiss, my peach!'

Zeitlin closed his eyes and kissed Andronnikov on the rouged lips. Anything for Sashenka, he thought. 'Lovely party, My Prince.'

'Too hot, too hot,' said the Prince gravely – adding 'too hot for clothes, eh?' to the youth next to him, who chortled. The red silk walls were crammed with signed photographs of ministers and generals and grand dukes: was there anyone who did not owe Andronnikov something? Entrepreneur of influence, gutter journalist, friend of the powerful and poisonous gossip, Andronnikov helped set the prices in the Bourse of influence, and had just brought down the War Minister.

'My Prince, it's about my daughter . . .' Zeitlin began – but a more aggressive petitioner, a skinny ginger-haired woman with freckles and an ostrich feather rising out of a peacock brooch on a silk turban, interrupted him. Her son needed a job at the Justice Ministry but was already on a train out to the Galician Front. Protopopov, the Interior Minister, could see the price for this favour dangling before him and rose, taking the lady's hand. Zeitlin saw his chance and moved into the vacated seat next to Andronnikov, who inclined his head and put his hand on his famous white briefcase, a mannerism that meant: let us deal.

'Dear Prince, my daughter Sashenka . . .'

Andronnikov waved a spongy jewelled hand. 'I know . . . your daughter at Smolny . . . arrested this afternoon – and guilty by all accounts. Well, I don't know. What do you suggest?'

'She's at the Kresty Temporary House of Detention right now: can we get her out tonight?'

'Easy now, dearie! It's a bit late for tonight, sweetheart. But we wouldn't want her to get three years in Yeniseisk on the Arctic Circle, would we?'

Zeitlin had palpitations at the thought: his darling Sashenka would never survive that! Andronnikov sank into an open-mouthed kiss with the youth next to him. When he came up for air, his lips still wet, Zeitlin pointed at the ceiling.

'My Prince, I'd like to buy your . . . chandelier,' he suggested. 'I've always admired it . . .'

'It's very close to my heart, Baron. A present from the Empress herself.'

'Really? Well, let me make you an offer for it. Shall we say at least . . .'

CHAPTER 12

Ariadna's companion for her nocturnal voyage from Baroness Rozen's salon and on to dinner was Countess Missy Loris, a cheerful blonde born in America but married to a Russian. Missy had begged Ariadna to introduce her to Rasputin, who, it was said, was virtually ruling Russia.

Holding Missy's hand, Ariadna dismounted from the Russo-Balt limousine and passed through the shadowy archway of 64 Gorokhovaya Street, across an asphalt courtyard and up the steps of a red three-storey building. The door opened as if by magic. A doorman – unmistakably ex-military, surely an agent of the Okhrana – bowed. 'Second floor.'

The women walked up the stairs towards an open doorway lined in scarlet silk. A red-faced man in blue serge trousers and braces, clearly a policeman, pointed them inside brusquely. 'Ladies, this way!'

A squat peasant woman in a floral dress took their coats and showed them into a room where a tall silver samovar bubbled and steamed. Beside it, and toying with handfuls of silks, chinchilla and sable furs, diamonds and egret feathers, sat the Elder Grigory, known as Rasputin, in a lilac silk shirt tucked into a crimson sash, striped trousers, and kid leather boots. His face was weathered, moley and wrinkled, his nose pockmarked, his hair centre-parted into greasy bangs that formed arches on his forehead, and his beard was reddish brown. Yellow eyes gazed up at Ariadna without blinking, the glazed pupils flickering from side to side as if they saw nothing.

'Ah, my Little Bee,' he said. 'Here!' He offered his hand to the women. Ariadna tipsily fell on one knee and kissed the hand, which moved on to Missy. 'I know what you've come about. Go into my reception room. My little doves are all here, dear Bee. And you're new.' He squeezed Missy's waist, which tickled her, and she squealed. 'Show her round, Little Bee.'

'Little Bee,' whispered Ariadna to Missy, 'is his special name for me. We all have nicknames.'

'Don't forget to mention Sashenka.'

'Sashenka, Sashenka. There, I'm remembering.'

The pair entered the main room, where ten or so guests, mostly women, sat round a table covered in their offerings – a heap of black Beluga caviar, half a sturgeon in aspic, piles of peppermint gingersnaps, boiled eggs, a coffee cake and a bottle of Cahors.

Rasputin was right behind them. He put his arm around Ariadna's waist and swung her round, steering her to a seat at the table. He greeted them separately. 'Wild Dove, meet Little Bee, Pretty Dandy, the Calm One . . .'

Among the women sat a plump moon-faced blonde in a drab, badly ironed and poorly made beige dress – and a treble string of the biggest pearls that Ariadna had ever seen. This shiny-cheeked creature was Anna Vyrubova, and the pretty, dark lady next to her, wearing a fashionable sailor-suit dress and a black and white bonnet, was Julia 'Lili' von Dehn: these, Ariadna knew, were the Empress's two best friends. The spirituality of the atmosphere was intensified by the exalted status of those present. Ariadna was keenly aware that, with the Emperor away at the front, the Empress ruled the Empire through the people in this room. She knew that Missy was not yet a devotee of the Elder – in fact she was there for the party. She was bored with sweet, banal Count Loris and adored anything that was fashionable or outré – and this was both. But for Ariadna it was different. Already drunk and high, she felt cleansed in this room. Whoever she was outside, however unhappy and insecure she felt at home, however desperate her love affairs and random her search for meaning in the universe, here things had a calm simplicity that she had never found before.

Rasputin walked around the table so that each guest might kiss his hand. When he found an empty chair, he sat down and took a handful of sturgeon in his bare fist and started to eat, smearing the food in his beard. The ladies watched in silence as he gobbled handfuls of cake, fish, caviar, without the slightest self-consciousness, his chomping loud and hearty. When he was finished, he gazed at them all and then placed his hands on Ariadna's hands and squeezed them.

'You! Honeyed friend, you need me most tonight and I'm here.'

A blushing glow started on Ariadna's chest and rose up her neck and throughout her body, as if she felt something between teenage bashfulness, religious awe and sensual excitement. Vyrubova's bulging eyes, crafty yet credulous, glared jealously at her. What does our Friend see in this lowborn *zhyd*, the Jew banker's sluttish wife? Ariadna knew she was thinking – even though Vyrubova herself, and the Empress too, had benefited from Zeitlin's generosity.

Ariadna did not care even though the ugly flush was covering her neck and bare shoulders. Here she was no longer a *Yiddeshe dochte* born Finkel Barmakid in the court of the famous rabbi of Turbin, or the troubled neurasthenic who could barely control her appetites. Here she was a woman worthy to be loved and cherished – even among the friends of the Tsars themselves. Rasputin talked to empresses and whores as though they were the same. This was the Elder's genius – he made his bewildered doves into proud lionesses, his neurasthenic victims into beautiful champions. This sacred peasant would save Russia, the Tsars, the world. Ariadna's breath hissed between her teeth; her tongue darted out to lick her dry lips. The room was quiet except for the murmur of the Elder and the humming of the samovar next door.

'Little Bee,' he said quietly in his simple country accent, raising her and leading her around the table to the sofa against the wall where he sat her down, pulling up his chair, squeezing her legs between his own. A tremor ran through her. 'You have an emptiness inside you. You're always balanced between despair and a void within. You're a Hebrew? You're a troublesome people but much wronged too. I will keep you all out of trouble. Just follow my holy way of love. Don't listen to your priests or rabbis' – he took in her shiny eyes in a single glance – 'they don't know the whole mystery. Sin is given so that we may repent and repentance brings joy to the soul and strength to the body, understand?'

'We do, we do understand,' said Vyrubova in a loud, crude voice behind Rasputin.

'How is brutalized man with his beast's habits to climb out of the pit of sin and live a life pleasing to God? Oh you are my darling, my Honey Bee.' His face was so close to hers that Ariadna could smell the sturgeon and the Madeira wine on his breath, the scent on his beard and the alcohol in his sweat. 'Sin should be understood. Without sin there is no life because there is no repentance and if there is no repentance there is no joy. How are you looking at me, Little Bee?'

'With holiness, Father. I have sinned,' she started. 'I'd die without love. I need to be loved at every moment.'

'You're thirsty, Honey Bee.' He kissed her lips very slowly. 'For now, Honey Bee, come with me. Let us pray.' Leaving the other women behind, he took her hand and let her through the curtain into the sanctum.

CHAPTER 13

Sashenka's jailhouse dawn was a blinding light and the heady fumes of a long night's distilled urine as every woman in the cell emptied her bladder in turn. Her Smolny pinafore was wet and bloodstained and she ached in every fibre of her body. Boots on stone, the turning of keys and screeching of locks. The cell door swung open.

A man stood in the doorway. 'Ugh! It's rank in here,' he muttered then pointed at Sashenka. 'That's the one. Bring her.'

Natasha squeezed her hand as two warders waded through the sprawled bodies and fished her out of the cell. They manhandled her through the grey corridors and deposited her in an interrogation room with a plain desk, a metal chair and walls peeling with damp. She could hear a man crying next door.

A gendarme, a lieutenant with a square head, shaven close, and a long square-cut beard, opened the door, stalked up to her and banged his fist on the table.

'You're going to tell us every single name,' he

said, 'and you're never going to fuck around like this again.' Sashenka flinched as he hoisted himself on to the table's edge and pushed his livid face up close to hers. 'You've every advantage in life,' he shouted. 'True, you're not a real Russian. You're a *zhyd*, you're not nobility. Your Jew father probably salutes the Kaiser every night . . .'

'My father's a Russian patriot! The Tsar gave him a medal!'

'Don't answer me like that. That title of his ain't a Russian title. Jews can't have titles here. Everyone knows that. He bought it with stolen roubles from some German princeling . . .'

'The King of Saxony made him a baron.' Whatever Sashenka's views on her father's class and the capitalist war, she was still his daughter. 'He works hard for his country.'

'Shut up unless you want a slap. Once a *zhyd* always a *zhyd*. Profiteers, revolutionaries, tinkers. You *Evrei* – Hebrews – are all at it, aren't you? But you're such a looker. Yes, you're real fresh strawberries!'

'How dare you!' she said quietly, always uneasy about her appearance. 'Do not speak to me like that!'

Sashenka had not eaten or drunk since the night before. After her brave moments of defiance, her courage and energy were draining away. She needed food like the furnace of an engine needs coal, and she longed for a hot bath. Yet as she listened to the bully shouting at her, he began to lose his power. She did not fear his small pink eyes and the blue uniform of a degenerate system. The spray of his spittle was grotesque but easily wiped away.

She closed her eyes for a second, removing herself from this police bully, this Derzhimorda. Not for the first time, she imagined the effect of her arrest at home. My dear distant father, where are you at this moment? she wondered. Am I just another problem for you to solve? What about Fanny Loris and the girls at school? How I'd love to hear their trivial chatter today. And my darling Lala, kind, thoughtful Mrs Lewis with the lullaby voice. She does not know that the girl she loves no longer exists . . .

The shouting came closer again. Sashenka felt faint with hunger and fatigue as the interrogator filled in his forms in brutish semiliterate squiggles. Name? Age? Nationality? Schooling? Parents? Height? Distinguishing features? He wanted her fingerprints: she gave him her right hand. He pressed each finger down on an inkpad and then on to his form.

'You'll be charged under Paragraph One, Article 126, for being a member of the illegal Russian Socialist Democratic Workers' Party, and Paragraph One, Article 102, for being a member of a military organization. Yes, little girl, your friends are terrorists, murderers, fanatics!'

Sashenka knew this was all about the pamphlets she had been distributing for her uncle Mendel.

Who wrote them? Where was the printing press? the man asked, again and again.

'Did you handle the "noodles" and the "bulldogs"?'

'Noodles? I don't know what you mean.'

'Don't play the innocent with me! You know perfectly well that noodles are belts of ammunition for machine guns, and bulldogs are pistols, Mauser pistols.'

Another shower of saliva.

'I'm feeling faint. I think I need to eat . . .' she whispered.

He stood up. 'All right, princess, we're having a funny turn, are we? A swoon like that countess in *Onegin*?' He scraped back his chair and took her elbow roughly. 'Captain Sagan will see you now'.

CHAPTER 14

'Greetings, Mademoiselle Baroness,' said the officer just down the corridor, in a tidy office that smelled of sawdust and cigars. 'I am Captain Sagan. Peter Mikhailovich de Sagan. I do apologize for the bad manners – and breath – of some of my officers. Here, sit down.'

He stood up and looked at his new prisoner: a slim girl with luxuriant brown hair stood before him in a crumpled and stained Smolny uniform. He noticed that her lips, in contrast to her pale, bruised face, were crimson and slightly swollen. She stood awkwardly, her arms crossed tightly over her chest, looking down at the floor.

Sagan bowed, neat in his white-trimmed blue tunic, boot heels together, as if they were at a soirée and then offered his hand. He liked to shake his prisoners' hands. It was one way of 'taking their temperature' and showing what the general called 'Sagan's steel under the charm'. He noticed this girl's hands were shaking and that she carried the noxious smell of the cells. Was that blood on her Smolny pinafore? Some crazy hag had probably attacked her. Well, this was not the Yacht Club. Posh schoolgirls should think of such things before conspiring against their Emperor.

He pulled a chair over and helped her to sit. His first impression was that she was absurdly young. But Sagan liked to say he was 'a professional secret policeman, not a nurse'. There were opportunities for him among those who were absurdly young and spoilt and out of their depth. Insignificant as she was, she must know something. She was Mendel's niece after all.

She flopped into the chair. Sagan noted her exhaustion with satisfaction – and calibrated pity. She was really no more than a confused child. Still, it opened up interesting possibilities.

'You look hungry, mademoiselle. Fancy ordering some breakfast? Ivanov?' A gendarme NCO appeared in the doorway.

She nodded, avoiding his eyes.

'What can I get you, maga-mozelle?' Ivanov flourished an imaginary pen and paper, playing the French waiter.

'Let's see!' Captain Sagan answered for her, remembering the reports in the surveillance files. 'I'll bet you have hot cocoa, white bread lightly toasted, saltless butter and caviar for breakfast?' Sashenka nodded mutely. 'Well, we can't do the caviar but we have cocoa, bread and I did find a little Cooper's Fine Cut Marmalade from Yeliseyev's on Nevsky Prospect. Any good to you?'

'Yes, please.'

'You've been bleeding.'

'Yes.'

'Someone attacked you?'

'Last night, it was nothing.'

'Do you know why you're here?'

'I was read the charges. I'm innocent.'

He smiled at her but she still did not look at him. Her arms remained crossed and she was shivering.

'You're guilty of course, the question is how guilty.'

She shook her head. Sagan decided this was going to be a very dull interrogation. Ivanov, wearing an apron stretched lumpily over his blue uniform, wheeled in the breakfast and offered bread, marmalade and some cocoa in a mug.

'Just as you ordered, maga-mozelle,' he said.

'Very good, Ivanov. Your French is exquisite.' Sagan turned to his prisoner. 'Does Ivanov remind you of the waiters at the Donan, your papa's favourite, or the Grand Hotel Pupp at Carlsbad?'

'I've never stayed there,' Sashenka whispered, running her fingertips over her wide lips, a gesture she made, he noticed, when she was thoughtful. 'My mother stays there: she puts me and my governess in a dingy boarding house. But you knew that.' She was silent again.

They're always the same. Unhappy at home, they get mixed up in bad company, he thought. She must be starving, but he would wait for her to ask him whether she could eat.

Instead she suddenly looked straight up at him as if the sight of the food had already restored her. Grey eyes, cool as slate, examined him. The speckled lightness of the irises – grains of gold amid the grey – under the hooded eyebrows, projecting a mocking curiosity, took him aback.

'Are you going to sit there and watch me eat?' she asked, taking a piece of bread.

First point to her, thought Sagan. The gentleman in him, the descendant of generations of Baltic barons and Russian generals, wanted to applaud her. Instead he just grinned.

She picked up a knife, spread the bread with butter and marmalade and ate every piece, quickly and neatly. He noticed there were delicate freckles on either side of her nose, and now her arms were no longer crossed he could see that she had a most abundant bosom. The more she tried to hide her breasts, the more conspicuous they became. We interrogators, concluded Sagan, must understand such things.

Ivanov removed the plates. Sagan held out a packet of cigarettes emblazoned with a crocodile.

'Egyptian gold-tipped Crocodiles?' she said.

'Aren't they your only luxury?' he replied. 'I know that Smolny girls don't smoke but in prison, who's watching?' She took one and he lit it for her. Then he took one himself and threw it spinning into the air, catching it in his mouth.

'A performing monkey as well as a torturer,' she said in her soft voice with its bumble-bee huskiness, and blew out smoke in blue rings. 'Thanks for breakfast. Am I going home now?'

Ah, decided Sagan, she does have some spirit after all. The light caught a rich tinge of auburn in her dark hair.

Sagan reached for a pile of handwritten reports.

'Are you reading someone's diary?' she asked, cheekily.

He looked up at her witheringly. 'Mademoiselle, your life as you knew it is over. You will probably be sentenced by the Commission to the maximum five years of exile in Yeniseisk, close to the Arctic Circle. Yes, *five* years. You may never come back. The harsh sentence reflects your treason during wartime and, as you are a Jew, next time it will harsher still.'

'Five years!' Her breaths grew quick and shallow. 'It's *your* war, Captain Sagan, a slaughter of working men on the orders of emperors and kings, not *our* war.'

'OK, here's the game. These are the surveillance reports of my agents. Let me read what my files say about a certain person I will call Madame X. You have to guess her real name.' He took a breath, his eyes twinkling, then lowered his voice theatrically. '*After following the erotic religion of Arzabyshev's novel* Sanin *and taking part in sexual debauchery, she embraced the "Eastern" teachings of the so-called healer Madame Aspasia del Balzo, who revealed through a process called spiritual retrogression that in a former life Mrs X had been the hand-maiden of Mary*

Magdalene and then the bodice-designer of Joan of Arc.'

'That's too easy! Madame X is my mother,' said Sashenka. Her nostrils flared and Sagan noticed her lips never quite seemed to close. He turned back to his file.

'*In a table-turning session, Madame Aspasia introduced Baroness Zeitlin to Julius Caesar, who told her not to allow her daughter Sashenka to mock their psychic sessions.*'

'You're making it up, Captain,' said Sashenka drily.

'In the lunatic asylum of Piter, we don't need to make anything up. You appear quite often in this file, mademoiselle, or should I say Comrade Zeitlin. Here we are again. *Baroness Zeitlin continues to pursue any road to happiness offered to her. Our investigations reveal that Madame del Balzo was formerly Beryl Crump, illegitimate daughter of Fineas O'Hara Crump, an Irish undertaker from Baltimore, whereabouts unknown. After embracing the teachings of the French hierophant doctor Monsieur Philippe and then the Tibetan healer Dr Badmaev, Baroness Zeitlin is now a follower of the peasant known to his adepts as "Elder", whom she asked to exorcize the evil spirits of her daughter Sashenka who she says despises her and has destroyed her spiritual well-being.*'

'You've made me laugh under interrogation,' Sashenka said, looking solemn. 'But don't think that you've got me that easily.'

Sagan spun the file on to his desk, sat back and

held up his hands. 'Apologies. I wouldn't for a second underestimate you. I admired your article in the illegal *Rabochnii Put – Workers' Path* – newspaper.' He drew out a grubby tabloid journal headed with a red star. 'Title: "The Science of Dialectical Materialism, the Cannibalistic Imperialist Civil War, and Menshevik Betrayal of the Proletarian Vanguard"'.

'I never wrote that,' she protested.

'Of course not. But it's very thorough and I understand from one of our agents in Zurich that your Lenin was quite impressed. I don't imagine any other girls at the Smolny Institute could write such an essay, quoting from Plekhanov, Engels, Bebel, Jack London and Lenin – and that's just the first page. I don't mean to patronize.'

'I said I didn't write it.'

'It's signed *Tovarish Pesets. Comrade Snowfox.* Your shadows tell me you always wear an Arctic fox fur, a gift from an indulgent father perhaps?'

'A frivolous *nom de révolution*. Not mine.'

'Come on, Sashenka – if I may call you that. No man would choose that name: we've got Comrade Stone – Kamenev, and Comrade Steel – Stalin, both of whom I have personally despatched to Siberia. And Comrade Molotov – the Hammer. Do you know their real names?'

'No, I—'

'Our Special Section knows everything about your Party. It's riddled with our informers. So back to "Comrade Snowfox". Not many women in the Party could carry it off. Alexandra Kollontai perhaps, but we know her revolutionary code-name. Anyway she's in exile and you're here. By the way, have you read her *Love of the Worker Bees?*'

'Of course I have,' Sashenka replied, sitting up straight. 'Who hasn't?'

'But I imagine all that free love is more your mother's style?'

'What my mother does is her own business, and as to my private life, I don't have one. I don't want one. All *that* disgusts me. I despise such trivia.'

The ash-grey eyes looked through him again. There is no one as sanctimonious as a teenage idealist (especially one who is a rich banker's precious daughter), reflected Sagan. He was impressed with her game, yet was not quite sure what to do: should he release her or keep working on her? She might just be the minnow to hook some bigger fish.

'You know your parents and uncle Gideon Zeitlin all tried to get you released last night.'

'Mama? I'm surprised she'd bother . . .'

'Sergeant Ivanov! Have you got last night's report from Rasputin's place?' Ivanov clomped into the room with the file. Sagan leafed quickly through handwritten papers. 'Here we are. *Report of Agent Petrovsky: Dark One* – that's our codename for Rasputin in case you hadn't guessed – *talked to Ariadna Zeitlin, Jewess, wife of the industrialist, and acknowledged she had a special subject to discuss. But after a private session with the Dark One on the subject of sin and an unruly scene on the arrival of Madame Lupkina, Zeitlin, accompanied by the American Countess Loris, left the Dark One's apartment at 3.33am and was driven to the Aquarium nightclub and then the Astoria Hotel, Mariinsky Square, in the same Russo-Balt landaulet motor car. Both appeared intoxicated. They visited the suite of Guards Captain Dvinsky, cardsharp and speculator, where . . . champagne ordered . . . blah, blah . . . they left at 5.30am. The Jewess Zeitlin's stockings were torn and her clothes were in a disordered state. She was driven back to the Zeitlin residence in Greater Maritime Street and the car then conveyed the American to her husband's apartment on Millionaya, Millionaires' Row . . .'*

'But . . . she never mentioned me?'

Sagan shook his head. 'No – although her American friend did. Your father was more effective. But,' he raised a finger as her face lit up in expectation, 'you're staying right here. Only as a favour to you, of course. It would ruin your credibility with your comrade revolutionaries if I released you too soon.'

'Don't be ridiculous.'

'If I do release you now, they may think you've become one of my double agents – and then they'd have to rub you out. Don't think they'd be kinder because you're a schoolgirl. They're ice cold. Or they'd assume your rich parents scurried to Rasputin or Andronnikov and bought you out.

They'd think – quite rightly in my view – that you're just a frivolous dilettante. So I'll be doing you a favour when I make sure you get those five years in the Arctic.'

He watched the flush creep up her neck, flood her cheeks and burn her temples. She's frightened, he thought, pleased with himself.

'That would be an honour. *I'm brave and fear neither knife nor fire,*' she said, quoting Zemfira in Pushkin's 'Gypsies'. 'Besides, I'll escape. Everyone does.'

'Not from there you won't . . . Zemfira. It's more likely you'll die up there. You'll be buried by strangers in a shallow unmarked grave on the taiga. You'll never lead any revolutions, never marry, never have children – your very presence on this earth a waste of the time, money and care your family have expended on it.'

He saw a shudder pass right through her from shoulder to shoulder. He allowed the silence to develop.

'What do you want from me?' she asked, her voice shrill with nerves.

'To talk. That's all,' he said. 'I'm interested in your views, Comrade Snowfox. In what someone like you thinks of this regime. What you read. How you see the future. The world's changing. You and I – whatever our beliefs – are the future.'

'But you and I couldn't be more different,' she exclaimed. 'You believe in the Tsars and landowners and exploiters. You're the secret fist of this disgusting empire, while I believe it's doomed and soon it'll come crashing down. Then the people will rule!'

'Actually we'd probably agree on many things, Sashenka. I too know things must change.'

'History will change the world as surely as the sun rises,' she said. 'The classes will vanish. Justice will rule. The Tsars, the princes, my parents and their depraved world, and nobility like you . . .' She stopped abruptly as if she had said too much.

'Isn't life strange? I shouldn't be saying this at all but we probably want the same things, Sashenka. We probably even read the same books. I adore Gorky and Leonid Andreyev. And Mayakovsky.'

'But I love Mayakovsky!'

'I was in the Stray Dog cellar bar the night he declaimed his poems – and do you know, I wept. I wasn't in uniform of course! But yes, I wept at the sheer courage and beauty of it. You've been to the Stray Dog of course?'

'No, I haven't.'

'Oh!' Sagan feigned surprise with a fleck of disappointment. 'I don't suppose Mendel is too interested in poetry.'

'He and I don't have time to visit smoky cabarets,' she said, sulkily.

'I wish I could take you,' he told her. 'But you said you loved Mayakovsky? My real favourite is

'Whorehouse after whorehouse
With six-storey-high fauns daring dances . . .'

– and she took up the poem, enthusiastically:

'Stage Manager! The hearse is ready
Put more widows in the crowds!
There aren't enough there!
No one ever asked
That victory be'

– and Sagan picked up the verse again:

'Inscribed for our homeland
To an armless stump left from the bloody banquet.
What the hell good is it?'

Sashenka marked the rhythm with both hands, flushed with the passion of the words. A vision, thought Sagan, of rebellious, defiant youth.

'Well, well, and I thought you were just a silly schoolgirl,' he said, slowly.

There was a knock on the door. Ivanov strode in and gave Sagan a note. He rose briskly and tossed his files on to his desk, sending the particles of dust, suspended in the sunlight, into little whirlwinds.

'Well,' said Sagan, 'that's that. Goodbye.'

Sashenka seemed indignant. 'You're sending me back? But you haven't even asked me anything.'

'When did your uncle Mendel Barmakid recruit

you to the Russian Socialist Democratic Workers'
Party? May 1916. How did he escape from exile?
By reindeer sleigh, steamship, train (second-class
ticket, no less). Don't worry your pretty eyes,
Comrade Snowfox, we know it all. I'm not going
to waste any more time trying to interrogate you.'
Sagan pretended to be slightly exasperated while
actually he was well satisfied. He had got exactly
what he wanted from their meeting. 'But I've
enjoyed our conversation greatly. I think we should
talk about poetry again very soon.'

CHAPTER 15

Sashenka swathed herself in her snowfox stole and Orenburg shawl as the chief warder held open her sable coat. Stepping into its sleek silk-lined warmth was like sinking into a bath of warm milk. She shivered at the pleasure of it, scarcely aware of the warblings of Sergeant Volkov about 'politicals' and 'criminals', Swiss chocolates and Brocard's cologne (which he had applied liberally for just this moment).

Sashenka's arrival at the Kresty seemed decades ago, not just the previous night. And when the sergeant said, 'You see, I'm not your typical prison warder,' she suddenly wanted to hug him. He handed her the canvas book bag.

As she left the prison, she felt she was floating on air. Warders bowed. Door after door opened, bringing the light closer. Gendarmes wielded giant keys on swinging keyrings, locks ground open. The gendarme at the counter actually touched the brim of his cap. Everyone seemed to wish her well, as if she was a scholar leaving a school for the last time.

Who would meet her? she wondered. Papa? Flek,

the family lawyer? Lala? But before she could even formulate a prediction, Uncle Gideon was opening his strapping arms at full span and dancing towards her, almost falling sideways as if the world was tilting. He wrapped her in his fur, his beard scratching her neck, almost lifting her off the ground.

'Oh my heart!' he bellowed, regardless of the gendarmes. 'There she is! Come on! Everyone's waiting!' At that moment, she loved his cognac-and-cigars scent and inhaled it hungrily.

And then she was outside in the freezing light of northern winter. Her father's Russo-Balt landaulet, with chains on its wheels against the ice, lurched forward. Pantameilion, a flash of scarlet and gold braid, ran round to open the door and Sashenka almost collapsed into that leather-lined, sweet-smelling compartment with its fresh carnations in the silver vase. Lala's arms enveloped her and Uncle Gideon climbed into the front seat, swigged some brandy from his flask and took up the speaking tube.

'Home, Pantameilion, you young ladykiller! Fuck Mendel! Fuck the Revolution and all the ideeeots!' Lala rolled her eyes and the two women laughed.

As they crossed the bridge, Lala handed Sashenka the tin of Huntley & Palmers and her babushka Miriam's Yiddish honeycakes. She ate every delicacy, thinking that she had never so loved the spire of the Admiralty, the rococo glory of the

Winter Palace – and the golden dome of St Isaac's. She was going home. She was free!

Uncle Gideon threw open the door at Greater Maritime Street as Sashenka, running up the steps, rushed past Leonid, the old butler who, with tears in his eyes, bowed low from the waist like a village *muzhik* before his young mistress. Gideon tossed his shaggy furs at the butler, who almost crumpled under the weight, and demanded one of the footmen help him pull off his boots.

Sashenka, feeling like the little girl who was occasionally presented to her busy father, ran to his study. The door was open. She prayed he was there. She did not know what she would do if he wasn't. But he was. Zeitlin, in winged collar and spats, was listening to Flek.

'Well, Samuil, the prison governor demanded four hundred,' said the toad-like family lawyer.

'Small change compared with Andronnikov . . .' But then Zeitlin saw her. 'Thank God, you're here, my darling Lisichka-sestrichka – Little Fox Sister!' he said, reverting to one of her childhood nicknames. He opened his arms and she leaned into him, feeling his tidy moustache on her cheek, bathing in his familiar cologne, pressing her lips against his slightly rough skin. 'Let's get your coat off before we talk,' he said, releasing himself from her arms and leading her into the hall. Leonid, following dutifully in her wake, removed her coat, stole and shawl, and then she noticed her father was looking her up and down distastefully, his nostrils twitching. Sashenka had quite forgotten that she was still wearing her soiled Smolny pinafore. Suddenly she could smell the filth of prison that clung about her.

'Oh Sashenka, is that blood?' her father exclaimed.

'Oh dearest, we must get you bathed and changed,' cried Lala in her high breathy voice. 'Luda, draw a bath at once.'

'Sashenka,' murmured Zeitlin. 'Thank God we got you out.'

She yearned to wash yet she stood still, revelling in the shock of her father and the servants. 'Yes!' she proclaimed, her voice breaking. 'I've been to prison, I've seen the tombs that are the Tsar's jails. I'm no longer the Smolny girl you thought I was!'

In the silence that followed, Lala took Sashenka's hands and led her upstairs to the third floor, which was their own country. Up here, every worn piece of carpet, every crack on the landing walls, the damp stain on the pink wallpaper of her bedroom with its playful pictures of ponies and rabbits, the yellowed enamel of the basin in her English washstand, reminded Sashenka of her childhood with Lala, who had decorated her room to create a loving sanctuary for an only child.

The landing already smelt of Pears pine bath essence and Epsom Salts. Lala brought her straight into the bathroom, which was lined with the most indulgent British toiletry products, beautiful blue and amber and green bottles of lotions and oils and essences. The chunky bar of Pears soap, black, cracked, beloved, waited on the wooden bathrack.

'What are we having today?' asked Sashenka.

'Same as always,' replied Lala. Sashenka, even though she now regarded herself as an adult, did not resist as Lala undressed her and handed her stinking clothes to Luda.

'Burn them, will you, girl,' Lala said.

Sashenka loved the feel of the soft carpet under her feet and the misty essences curling around her. She glanced at her nakedness in the foggy mirror and winced at a body she preferred not to see as Lala helped her into the bath. The waters were so hot, the bath (English again, imported from Bond Street) so deep that immediately she closed her eyes and lay back.

'Darling Sashenka, I know you're tired,' said Lala, 'but just tell me, what happened? Are you all right? I was so worried . . .' And she burst into tears, large teardrops trickling down her wide cheeks.

Sashenka sat up and kissed the tears away. 'Don't worry, Lala. I was fine . . .' But as she settled into her bath, her mind travelled back to her final conversation with Mendel last summer holidays . . .

It had been *soomerki*, that beautiful word for

summer dusk. The oriole sang in the pine forests. Otherwise, it was quiet in the lilac light.

Sashenka had been lying in the hammock behind their house at Zemblishino, rocking gently and reading Mayakovsky's poetry to herself, when the sleepy swinging stopped. Mendel had his hand on the hammock.

'You're ready,' he said, sucking on a cigarette. 'When we get back to the city, you'll take on some workers' circles so you can teach them what you know. Then you'll join the Party.'

'Not just because I'm your niece?'

'Family and sentiment mean nothing to me,' he replied. 'What are such things compared to the course of history itself?'

'But what about Mama and Papa?'

'What about them? Your father is the arch exploiter and bloodsucker of the working class and your mother – yes, my own sister – is a degenerate haute bourgeoise. They're enemies of the science of history. They're irrelevant. Understand that and you're free of them for ever.'

He handed her a pamphlet with the same title as the first book he had given her weeks earlier: 'What Is to Be Done? Burning Questions of Our Party' by Lenin. 'Read it. You'll see that to be a Bolshevik is like being a knight in a secret military-religious order, a knight of the grail.'

And sure enough, in the weeks that followed, she had felt the joy of being an austere and merciless professional in Lenin's secret vanguard.

When she returned to the city, she began to lecture the workers' groups. She met ordinary workers, proletarians in the colossal Petrograd arms factories, men, women, even children, who possessed a gritty decency she had never encountered before. They slaved in dangerous factories and existed in airless grimy dormitories without bedding or baths or lavatories, without light or air, living like rats in a subterranean hell. And she met the workers who manufactured the rifles and howitzers that had made her own father a rich man. Daily, she worked with the most fiery and dedicated Party members who risked their lives for the Revolution. The clandestine world of committees, codes, conspiracy and comrades intoxicated her – and how could it not? It was the drama of history!

When she should have been at dance lessons or visiting Countess Loris's house to play with her friend Fanny, she started to act as Mendel's courier, carrying first leaflets and spare parts for printing presses but then 'apples' – grenades, 'noodles' – ammunition, and 'bulldogs' – pistols. While Fanny Loris and her schoolfriends composed scented letters in curling, girlish handwriting to young lieutenants in the Guards, Sashenka's billets-doux were notes with coded orders from 'Comrade Furnace', one of Mendel's codenames; and her polkas were rides on public trams or her father's sleigh bearing secret cargoes in her lingerie or her fur-collared *sluba* cape.

'You're the perfect courier,' said Mendel, 'because who would search a Smolny schoolgirl in a snowfox stole riding in a blood-sucker's crested sleigh?'

'Sashenka!' Lala was shaking her gently in her bath. 'It's lunchtime. You can sleep all afternoon. They're waiting for you.'

As Lala rubbed her back, Sashenka thought of her interrogation by Sagan, the whispers of Natasha, Mendel's woman, and her own ideals and plans. She realized she was stronger and older than she had been yesterday.

CHAPTER 16

Five minutes later, Sashenka stood at the door of the drawing room.

'Come in,' said her father, who was warming his back against the fire and smoking a cigar. Above him hung an Old Master painting of the founding of Rome set in a colossal gold frame.

She was surprised to see that the room was full of people. In Russian tradition, a nobleman held open house at lunchtime every day, and Zeitlin liked to play the nobleman. But she had expected her parents to cancel this mockery on the day she was released from prison. As she looked around the room, she wanted to cry – and she remembered a time when she was a little girl and her parents were giving a dinner party for the Minister of War, a Grand Duke and various grandees. That evening she had longed for her parents' attention, but when she appeared downstairs her father was in his study – 'I asked not to be interrupted, could you take her out please' – and her mother, in a beaded velvet gown with gilded acanthus leaves, was arranging the placement – 'Quick! Take her upstairs!' As she left, Sashenka secretly seized a crystal wine glass, and when, on the third floor, she heard the fuss as the Emperor's cousin arrived, she dropped it over the banisters and watched it shatter on the flagstones below. In the fracas that followed, her mother slapped her, even though her father had banned any punishment; and once again, Sashenka had found Lala her only source of comfort.

Sashenka recognized the inevitable Missy Loris (in an ivory-coloured brocade dress fringed with sable) talking to her husband, the simian but good-natured count. Gideon held up his glass for another cognac and addressed the lawyer Flek, whose bulging belly was pressed against the round table.

There was an English banker too – a friend of Ariadna and Mendel's long-departed brother, Avigdor, who had left in 1903 to make his fortune in London. Two members of the Imperial Duma, some of Zeitlin's poker cronies, a general in braid and shoulder-boards, a French colonel, and Mr Putilov, the arms manufacturer. Sashenka gave him a satisfied smile as she had spent many hours instructing his workers to destroy his bloodsucking enterprise.

'Would you like a glass of champagne, Sashenka?' her father offered.

'Lemon cordial,' she answered.

Leonid brought it.

'What's for lunch?' she asked the butler.

'The baron's favourite, Mademoiselle Sashenka:

Melba toast and terrine, blinis and caviar, Pojarsky veal cutlets cooked in sour cream with English Yorkshire pudding and *kissyel* cranberries in sugar jelly. The same as ever.'

But everything had changed, Sashenka thought. Can they not see that?

'A quick chat in my study first,' her father said.

I am to be tried, decided Sashenka, and then I shall have to talk to this bunch of shop dummies.

They went into the study. Sashenka remembered how, when her mother was away, her father would let her curl up in the cubby hole under the desk while he worked. She loved being near him.

'Can I listen?' It was Gideon who threw himself on to the sofa and lay back, sipping cognac. Sashenka was delighted he was there; he might help counteract her mother, who sat down opposite her, in her father's chair.

'Leonid, close the door. Thank you,' said Zeitlin, leaning on the Trotting Chair. 'Do sit.' Sashenka sat. 'We're so glad you're home, dear girl, but you did give us a hell of a shock. It wasn't easy getting you out. You should thank Flek.'

Sashenka said she would.

'You really might have been on your way to Siberia. The bad news is that you're not going back to Smolny . . .'

That's no funeral, thought Sashenka, that institute for imbeciles!

'. . . but we'll arrange tutoring. Well, you've shown us your independence. You've read your

Marx and Plekhanov. You've had a close shave. I was young once—'

'Were you?' asked Ariadna acidly.

'Not that I recall,' joked Gideon.

'Well, you may be right, but I went to meetings of *narodniks* and socialists in Odessa – once when I was very young. But this is deadly serious, Sashenka. There must be no more fooling around with these dangerous nihilists.' He came over and kissed the top of her head. 'I'm so glad you're home.'

'I'm so happy to be here, Papa.'

She gave him her hand and he pressed it, but Sashenka knew this loving scene with her father would provoke her mother. Sure enough, Ariadna cleared her throat.

'Well, you look quite unscathed. You've bored us long enough with your views on "workers" and "exploiters" and now you've caused us all a lot of trouble. I even had to bring this up with the Elder Grigory.'

Fury reared up inside Sashenka. She wanted to shout out that she was ashamed that a creature like Rasputin was ruling Russia, ashamed that her own mother, whose love affairs with cardsharps and fads with charlatans had long embarrased her, was now consorting with the Mad Monk. But instead, she could not stop herself answering like the petulant schoolgirl she still was. Searching for a target, she aimed for the dress chosen by her mother.

'Mama, I hate sailor suits and this is the last time I shall ever wear one.'

'Bravo!' said Gideon. 'A figure like yours is wasted in—'

'That's enough, Gideon. Please leave us alone,' said Ariadna.

Gideon got up to go, winking at Sashenka.

'You'll wear what I say,' said her mother, in her flowing crêpe-de-Chine dress with flounces of lace. 'You'll wear the sailor suits as long as you behave like an irresponsible child.'

'Enough, both of you,' Zeitlin said quietly. 'Your mother will indeed decide what you wear.'

'Thank you, Samuil.'

'But I propose a deal, darling girl. If you promise never to dabble in nihilism, anarchism and Marxism ever again, and never to talk politics with Mendel, your mother will take you shopping for your own adult gown at Chernyshev's, on my account. She'll let you have your hair done at Monsieur Troye's like her. You can get your cards and stationery printed at Treumann's and you and your mother can take Pantameilion and make "at home" calls. And you'll never have to dress in a sailor suit again.'

Zeitlin opened his hands, thought Sashenka, as if he had cut the Gordian knot or solved the mysteries of the Delphic oracle. She did not want dresses from Chernyshev's and she certainly did not need them where she was going. Her dear, silly father so longed for her to leave her cards and write love letters to pea-brained counts and guardsmen. But she already had what she needed: a plain high-necked blouse, a sensible skirt, woollen stockings and walking shoes.

'Agreed, Ariadna?'

Ariadna nodded and lit a Mogul cigarette. Then they both turned to Sashenka.

'Sashenka, look into my eyes and swear solemnly to this.'

Sashenka peered into her father's blue eyes and then glanced at her mother.

'Thank you, Papa. I promise that I will never ever talk politics with Mendel and never dabble in nihilism again.'

Zeitlin pulled a brocade cord.

'Yes, Baron,' replied Leonid, opening the door. 'Lunch is served.'

CHAPTER 17

A stunted man in pince-nez, an oversized coachman's sheepskin and a leather peaked cap with earmuffs stood on the Nevsky Prospect, watching the tramcar rumble towards him. It was dark, and a bitter blizzard whipped his face, already red and raw. The colossal General Staff building was on his left.

Mendel Barmakid looked behind him. The *shpik* – the secret-police spook – was still there, a moustachioed man with a military bearing in a green coat, trying to keep warm. Spooks tended to work in twos but he could not see the other one. Mendel was outside the illuminated windows of Chernyshev's, one of his sister's cheaper dressmakers. In a vitrine of mannequins in that season's velvet and tulle, he saw himself: a dwarf with a club foot, fat lips and a neat beard on the end of his chin. It was not an attractive sight but he had no time for sentimental indulgences. Nevsky was almost empty. The temperatures were falling – tonight it was minus 20 and the spooks had found him again when the Petrograd Committee met at the secret apartment in Vyborg. It was only ten days since his escape from exile, and now those police clots would debate whether to arrest him again or allow him to lead them to more comrades.

The tram stopped with a ringing of bells and a little meteor shower of sparks from the electric cables above. A woman got out. The spook beat his gloves together, his Cossack earring catching the light of the streetlamp.

The tram creaked forward. Suddenly Mendel ran towards it, his bad limp giving him a peculiar gait. His body twisted like a human parabola but he ran very fast for a cripple. The tram was moving now. It was hard to run in the snow and even though Mendel did not look back, he knew that the young, fit spook had already spotted him and was giving chase. Mendel grabbed hold of the bar. The conductor, shouting, 'Well run, old man!' seized his other arm and pulled him up.

Sweating inside his sheepskin, Mendel glanced back: the spook was running behind – but he was not going to make it. Mendel saluted him, noble-style, touching his brim.

He travelled two stops, then slipped off the tram at the pink Stroganov Palace and again checked his tails. No one – though they always found him again. He passed the colonnades of the Kazan Cathedral where he sometimes met comrades on the run from exile. The snow was slicing at the orange lanterns and he had to keep rubbing the lenses of his pince-nez. He saw only the shops of the bloodsucking classes – the Passazh with its expensive tailors and jewellers; the Yeliseyev Emporium with hams, sturgeons, cakes, oysters, clams, fancy teas and biscuits; the labyrinthine Gostiny Dvor, with its bearded merchants in kaftans selling antique icons and samovars; the English Shop with its Asprey bags and Fortnum & Mason fruitcakes.

Mendel heard the clipclop of horsemen – two gendarmes on patrol, but they were chatting to each other loudly about a whore in Kaluga and did not see him. He waited at the window of Yeliseyev's till they were gone. Then a Rolls-Royce sped by, and coming the other way a Delaunay: perhaps it was Zeitlin?

He reached the Hotel Europa, with its doormen in scarlet greatcoats and top hats. Its foyer and restaurant were the most heavily spied-upon square feet in the whole of Europe – and that was why he felt safe. No one would expect an escaped exile to linger here. But his coat was ragged and darned while the folk around here were in sables, frock coats, guardsmen's rig. Already the doorman, who was a police agent, was staring at him.

Mendel heard the dry swish of the sleigh. He limped over to a doorway to watch it come, searching for signs of *shpiki* and *fileri*, external agents. But the sleigh looked kosher, just one old hunched coachman.

Mendel hailed it and climbed in.

'Where to, sir?'

'The Taurida Palace.'

'Half a rouble.'

'Twenty kopeks.'

'The price of oats is up again. Can hardly feed the horse on that . . .'

Oats and more oats, thought Mendel. Prices were rising, the war was disastrous. But the worse, the better: that was his motto. The coachman, decided Mendel, was really a petit bourgeois with no role in the future. But then in Russia there were so few real proletarians on the Marxist model. Nine out of ten Russians were obstinate, backward, greedy, savage peasants. Lenin, with whom Mendel had shared sausages and beer in Cracow before the war, had mused that if the peasants did not accept the progress of history, their backs would have to be broken. 'Cruel necessity,' muttered Mendel.

Mendel was grey with exhaustion and mal-nutrition. It was hard to sleep, hard to eat on the run – yet somehow this existence suited him almost perfectly. No family – but then children bored him. Marriage – yes, but to Natasha the Yakut, another dedicated comrade whom he met only sporadically. Always on the move, he could sleep as easily on a park bench as on a floor or a divan. Lenin was in Switzerland and virtually the entire Central Committee – Sverdlov, Stalin, Kamenev – were in Siberia, and he was almost the last senior veteran of 1905 on the loose. But Lenin had ordered: 'You're needed in Piter: escape!' He had sent Mendel a hundred roubles to buy 'boots' – his false identity papers.

All that mattered was the Party and the cause: I am a knight of the holy grail with a broadsword in one hand and a book in the other, an armed slave to the Idea, Mendel thought, as the sleigh approached the domed portico, splendid Doric colonnade and ochre façade of the Taurida Palace, where the bourgeois saps of the talking-shop parliament – the Imperial Duma – now held their absurd debates. But before the sleigh was there, Mendel leaned forward and tapped the padded shoulder of the coachman.

'Here!' Mendel pressed some kopeks into the coachman's mitten and jumped off. Cars stood with their engines turning outside the Duma but Mendel did not approach the palace. Instead he limped into the lodge attached to the guardhouse of the Horse Guards Regiment next door. An old Adler limousine with the crest of a Grand Duke, bearing a Guards officer and a flunkey in court uniform, stopped and trumpeted its horn.

The gateman, simultaneously bowing, buttoning up his trousers and holding on to his hat, ran out and tried to open the gates. Mendel glanced around and knocked on the dusty door of the cottage.

The door opened. A ruddy-cheeked doorman in a Russian peasant smock and yellowed longjohns let him into a dreary little room with a stove, samovar and the fusty atmosphere of sleeping men and boiling vegetables.

'You?' said Igor Verezin. 'Thought you were in Kamchatka.'

'Yeniseisk Region. I walked.' Mendel noticed the doorman had a pointed bald pate the shape and colour of a red-hot bullet. 'I'm starving, Verezin.'

'*Shchi* soup, black Borodinsky bread and a sausage. The samovar's boiling, comrade.'

'Any messages for me?'

'Yes, someone pushed the newspaper through the door earlier.'

'Someone's coming tonight.'

Verezin shrugged.

'Where's the paper? Let me see. Good.' Mendel threw off his coat, checked the back window and the front. 'Can I sleep?'

'Be my guest, comrade. The sofa's yours though I might bed down myself there in a minute.' There was no bed in the dim little room and the doormen took turns sleeping on the divan. 'So how did you escape?'

But Mendel, still wearing his hat, boots and pince-nez, was already stretched out on the sofa.

There was a rap on the door, and the doorman found a teenage girl in a fine fur coat, undoubtedly sable, and a white fox-fur stole, who stepped hesitantly into the room. She was slim with a wide mouth and exceedingly light grey eyes.

'I'm in luck today!' joked Verezin. 'Excuse my pants!'

She gave him a withering look. '*Baramian*?' she asked.

'Get inside, milady,' joked Verezin, bowing like

a court flunkey. 'With that coat you should be going in the main gates with the field marshals and princes.'

Mendel stood up, yawning. 'Oh it's you,' he said, aware that his voice was his most impressive feature – deep and sonorous like a Jericho trumpet. He turned to Verezin. 'Could you take a walk? Round the block.'

'What? In this weather? You've got to be joking . . .' But Mendel never joked – except about the gallows. Instead the little man looked point-edly towards the stove behind which his 'bulldog' – a Mauser revolver – waited, wrapped in a cloth, and Verezin hurriedly changed his mind. 'I'll go and buy some salted fish.' Pulling on a greatcoat, he stomped outside.

When the doorman was gone, Sashenka sat down at the wicker table beside the stove.

'Don't you trust him?' She offered Mendel one of her perfumed Crocodile cigarettes with the gold tips.

'He's a concierge.' Mendel lit up. 'Most doormen are Okhrana informers – but when they sympa-thize with us they guard the safest safehouses. So as long as he doesn't turn, no one would look for a Bolshevik at the Horse Guards headquarters. He's a sympathizer and may join the Party.' He blew out a lungful of smoke. 'Your father's house is under surveillance. They're waiting for me. How did you get away?'

'I waited until everyone was asleep. Mama's out every night anyway. Then I used the Black Way into the courtyard and out through the garage. Trams, back doors, shops with two entrances, houses with courtyards. They never expect a girl in sable and kid boots to outwit them. You trained me well. I've learned the codes. I'm getting good at the craft. Like a ghost. And I'm fast as a mountain goat.'

Mendel felt an odd sensation, and realized he was happy to see her. She was sparkling with life. Yet he did not give her the hug he wanted to give her. The child was spoilt enough already.

'Don't get overconfident,' he said gruffly. 'Comrade Snowfox, did you deliver the message to the safehouse?'

'Yes.'

'Did you collect the pamphlets from the printing press?'

'Yes.'

'Where are they now?'

'In the apartment on the Petrograd Side. Shirokaya Street.'

'Tomorrow they need to reach the comrades at the Putilov Works.'

'I'll do it. Usual arrangements?'

Mendel nodded. 'You're doing well, comrade.'

She looked so young when she smiled, and by the dim lantern of the mean little room Mendel noticed the little shower of freckles on either side of her nose. He knew from her quick replies that she wanted to tell him something. He decided to make her wait.

Her intensity made him feel like an old man suddenly, conscious of his skin like porridge speckled with broken veins, of the strands of grey in his greasy hair, of the aches of his arthritis. That was what exile and prison did for you.

'Dear comrade,' she said, 'I can't thank you enough for your teaching. Now everything fits. I never thought the words "comrade" and "committee" would excite me so much, but they do. They really do!'

'Don't chatter too much,' he told her sternly. 'And watch yourself with comrades. They know your background and they look for signs of bourgeois philistinism. Change the sable. Get a karakul.'

'Right. I feel that I'm a cog in a secret world, in the universal movement of history.'

'We all are, but in Piter at the moment you're more important than you realize. We've so few comrades,' said Mendel, inhaling his cigarette, his red-rimmed eyes half closed. 'Keep reading, girl. You can't read enough. Self-improvement is the Bolshevik way.'

'The food shortages are getting worse. You've seen the queues? Everyone is grumbling – from the capitalists who come for lunch with Papa to comrades in the factories. Surely something will happen now?'

Mendel shook his head. 'One day, yes, but not now. Russia still lacks a real proletarian class and without one, revolution isn't possible. I'm not sure it'll happen in our lifetimes. How can one jump the stages of Marxist development? It can't happen, Sashenka. It's impossible.'

'Of course. But surely—'

'Even Lenin isn't sure we'll live to see it.'

'You get his letters?'

Mendel nodded. 'We've told him about the Smolny girl called Snowfox. How's the family?'

She took a breath. Here it comes, he thought.

'Comrade Mendel,' she said, 'I was arrested yesterday and spent the night at the Kresty.'

Mendel limped to the stove and, taking a greasy spoon, he leaned over the *shchi* soup and slurped a mouthful. The cigarette somehow remained hanging in the corner of his mouth.

'My first arrest, Uncle Mendel!'

He remembered his own first arrest twenty years ago, the appalled reaction of his father, the great Turbin rabbi, and his own pride on earning this badge of honour.

'Congratulations,' he told Sashenka. 'You're becoming a real revolutionary. Did the comrades of the cell committee take care of you?'

'Comrade Natasha looked after me. I didn't know you were married.'

Sometimes Sashenka was a real Smolny schoolgirl. 'I'm married to the Party. Comrades are arrested every day and very few are released the next morning.'

'There's something else.'

'Go on,' he said, leaning on the stove, an old exile's trick to ease the ache of Arctic winter. He

116

chomped on a hunk of cold sausage, cigarette miraculously still in position.

'I was interrogated for several hours by Gendarme Captain Peter Sagan.'

'Sagan, eh?' Mendel knew that Sagan was the Okhrana case officer tasked with finishing off the Party. He moved back to the little table, dragging his heavy boot. As he sat down, the table creaked. Now he was concentrating, watching her face. 'I think I've heard the name. What of him?'

'He was trying to lead me on, but Uncle Mendel,' she said, joining him at the table and gripping his arm, the Smolny schoolgirl again, 'he prides himself on his humanity. He's something of a bourgeois liberal. I know I'm a neophyte but I just wanted to inform you – and the Petrograd Committee – that he seemed keen to be my friend. Naturally I gave him no encouragement. But at the end, he said he would like to meet me again and continue our conversation—'

'—about what?'

'Poetry. Why are you smiling, Uncle Mendel?'

'You've done well, comrade,' Mendel said, thinking this new development through.

Sagan, a penniless nobleman, was a slick and ambitious policeman who specialized in turning female revolutionaries. But he might well be sympathetic to the Left, because the secret police knew how rotten the regime was better than anyone. It could be a signal, a trick, a seduction, a betrayal – or just an intellectually pretentious policeman. There were a hundred ways it could play out and Sashenka understood none of them, he thought.

'What if he *does* approach me?' she asked.

'What do you think?' answered Mendel.

'If he comes up to me in the street, I'll tell him never to talk to me again and curse him for good measure. Is that what you want me to do?'

Silence except for the flutter of the kerosene lamp. Mendel peered at her as intensely as a priest at an exorcism. The child he had known since her birth was an unfinished but very striking creature, he reflected, guessing that Sagan wanted to turn her into a double agent to get to Mendel himself. But there were two ways of playing this, and he could not miss a chance to destroy Sagan, whatever the cost.

'You're wrong,' he said slowly.

'If the committee wished it,' she said, 'I would kill him with Papa's Browning – it's in his desk – or there's the Mauser behind the bookcase at the safehouse on Shirokaya. Let me do it!'

'In the end, we'll put them *all* up against the wall,' said Mendel. 'Now, listen to me. You might never hear from Sagan again. But if he turns up, talk to him, draw him out. He could be helpful to the Party and to me.'

'What if he tries to recruit me?'

'He will. Let him think that's possible.'

'What if a comrade sees me with him?' she said anxiously.

'The Inner Bureau of the Committee will be informed of this operation. Three of us – a troika – just me and two others. Are you afraid?'

Sashenka shook her head. Her eyes were almost glowing in the dark. He could see she was scared and excited to have such a mission. 'But I could be killed by my own comrades as a traitor?'

'We're both in danger every minute,' he replied. 'The very second you become a Bolshevik, your normal life is over. You walk for ever on burning coals. It's like leaping on to a sleigh galloping so fast you can never get off. Chop wood and chips fly. We're in a secret war, the Superlative Game, you and I. The Party against the Okhrana. You do as I tell you, nothing more, and you report every word to me. You know the codes and the drops? Be vigilant. Vigilance is a Bolshevik virtue. You've become an asset to the Party quicker than I could have predicted. Understand?'

Mendel took care to moderate his voice and hoped he sounded convincing. He offered his hand and they shook. Her hand felt as silky, delicate and nervy as a little bird whose bones could be crushed with ease. 'Goodnight, comrade.'

Sashenka stood up and pulled on her coat, stole, boots and *shapka* and wrapped her head in the scarf. At the door she turned back, pale and serious.

'I'd hate you to protect me because I was family.'

'I never would, comrade.'

CHAPTER 18

'See the filly over there?' said the old coachman in the sheepskin, his cheeks as red as rare beef.

'Her again. Is she nursing a broken heart?'

'Is she a working girl or planning a bank robbery?'

'Perhaps she's booked a room at the hotel?'

'Is she slumming it for a lover who knows how to clean a horse's arse? Me, for example!'

'Hey, girl, have a vodka on us!'

In the middle of St Isaac's Square, not far from Greater Maritime Street, somewhere between the Mariinsky Palace and the cathedral, stood a flimsy wooden hut, painted black, with a tarpaulin roof so it looked like a giant one-horse cab with the hood up. Here in the bleary realm of overboiled cabbage and winter sweat, the coachmen of the one-horse cabs – the *izvoshtikis* – came to drink and eat in the early hours in a world beyond exhaustion.

Sashenka, a rough karakul coat and leather cap beside her, sat on her own, and put some kopeks into the noisy automatic barrel organ. It started to play 'Yankee Doodle' and then some Strauss waltzes and presently 'Yankee Doodle' again. Lighting a cigarette, she stared through the window at the Rolls-Royces outside the Astoria Hotel, the falling snow, and the horses tapping their hooves on the ice outside, waiting patiently, their breaths and whinnies all visible in the cold.

Two days had passed since her meeting with Mendel. At eleven that night, Lala had looked in on her in her bedroom.

'Turn your lights out now, darling,' she said. 'You look tired.' Lala sat on her bed and kissed her forehead as always. 'You'll hurt your eyes with all that reading. What are you reading about?'

'Oh Lala . . . one day I'll tell you,' Sashenka said, curling up to sleep, anxious that her governess should not discover that under the bed-clothes she was dressed ready to go out.

Once she knew Lala was asleep, she crept outside, taking a tram and then an *izvoshtik* over to the factories on the Petrograd Side. She spent an hour at the workers' circle at the Putilov and, together with another young intellectual, a boy from the Gymnasium, and a couple of lathe-turners, they delivered the spare parts for a printing press to a new hideout in Vyborg.

Afterwards she had an hour to kill so she walked along the Embankment and then along the Moika over her favourite little bridge, the Bridge of Kisses, past the ochre Yusupov Palace that more than any other building represented the iniquitous wealth of the few. She came here to the coachmen's hut because it was close to home – and yet in another dimension.

She ordered spicy *ukha* fish soup, goat's cheese, black Borodinsky bread and some tea – and sat listening to the men's gossip. When they talked about her as a dish, a looker, she did not quite understand what they meant. She could see her reflection in the little window and felt dissatisfied as always. She preferred to picture herself out in the freeze, buried in her high-necked coat, stole and *shapka*.

Cut out the vanity, Sashenka told herself. Her looks did not interest her. Like her uncle Mendel, she lived for the Revolution. Wherever she looked in the streets, she saw only those who would benefit from the beautiful march of the dialectic.

She dipped the bread and cheese into some mustard, and spluttered as the burn raced up her nose into her sinuses. Afterwards, she nibbled at a shapeless sugarlump and reflected that she was happier now than she had ever been in her entire life.

As a child, her parents had taken her to Turbin to visit the rabbinical court of her grandfather, Abram Barmakid, the saintly rabbi, with his beadles, disciples, students and hangers-on. She was very young and her father was not yet such a swell, and they lived in Warsaw, which was full of Hasidic Jews. But nothing had prepared Sashenka for the medieval realm of Abram Barmakid. The honest fanaticism, the rigid joy, even the guttural

Yiddish language, the men with ringlets, fringed shawls and gaberdine coats, the bewigged women – all of it scared her. Even then, she had feared their medieval spells and superstitions.

Yet she now reflected that her grandparents' world of golems and evil eyes was no worse than the secular money-worship of her father's market-place. Since childhood, she had been shocked by the injustices she had seen at Zemblishino and the manor house on his vast estates on the Dnieper. The luxury and debauchery of her parents' wretched marriage seemed to her to epitomize the rottenness of Russia and the capitalist world.

Mendel had rescued her from all this wicked-ness, and had changed her life. *If you love then love with verve; if you threaten mean it well*, the poet Alexei Tolstoy had written. That was her: '*All or nothing!*' She revelled in the delicious, almost amorous feeling of being part of a secret, a giant conspiracy. There was something seductive about sacrificing the old morality of the middle classes for the new morality of the Revolution. It was like sitting in this café: the very unromance of it was what made it so romantic.

She glanced at her watch. 4.45am. Time to go. She pulled on the coat and hat again, tossed down some coins. The coachmen watched, nodding at her. On the street, the draymen were delivering the milk crates, the patisserie van loading up with freshly baked bread. Carters dragged in sacks of coal. Janitors cleaned the steps. Piter was awakening.

123

The freezing air was so refreshing after the musk of the little hut that she inhaled it until it burned her lungs. How she loved Piter with its peculiar climate, almost arctic in its gummy winter blackness, but in summer, when it never grew dark, as bright as Paradise before the Fall. Its gorgeous facades in eggshell blue and ochre were magnificently imperial. But behind them were the factories, the electric trams, the yellow smoke and the crowded workers' dormitories. The beauty that surrounded her was a lie. The truth might seem ugly but it had its beauty too. Here was the future!

She crossed St Isaac's Square. Even in winter, you could spot the approach of dawn because the golden dome began to shine darkly long before there was as much as a glow on the horizon. The Astoria was still feasting – she could hear the band, glimpse in the gloom the diamonds of women, the orange tips of men's cigars. The Yacht Club was still open, troikas and limousines waiting outside for the courtiers and financiers.

She headed down Greater Maritime. She heard the rumble of a car and sank back into a doorway, like the ghost she had described to Mendel.

The Delaunay stopped outside her home. Pantameilion, in his long shining boots, opened the door of the car. Her mother climbed out. First one gorgeously clad foot in the softest kid boot appeared. Then a glimpse of silk stockings, then the satin dress, the sequins glittering.

A white hand studded with rings held the car's

doorframe. Sashenka was disgusted. Here she was, coming from serving the working class; here, with perfect symmetry, came her mother, fresh from servicing the desires of some corrupt man who was not her father.

Sashenka did not know what exactly it was that lovers did, though she knew it was like the dogs on her father's estate – and she was repulsed – yet rapt. She watched her mother pull herself out of the car and stand swaying. Pantameilion rushed to catch her hand.

Sashenka wanted to scratch her mother's face and throw her to the ground where she belonged, but she stepped out of the shadows to find Pantameilion crouched on the snow, pulling at a writhing sequinned form on the pavement. It was her mother struggling to get back on her feet.

Sashenka ran up to them. Ariadna was on all fours, her stockings torn and naked knees bleeding. She fell forward again, one gloved hand clawing at the snow, the other trying to fight off Pantameilion's proffered arm.

'Thanks, Pantameilion,' said Sashenka. 'Just check the doors are open. And send the watchman back to bed.'

'But miss, the baroness . . .'

'Please, Pantameilion, I'll look after her.'

Pantameilion's face bore the double anguish of servants faced with the collapse of their employers – they hated the topsy-turviness of a humiliated mistress just as they feared the insecurity of a fallen master. He bowed, shuffled into the house and emerged a moment later, climbing back into the growling Delaunay and jerking it into gear.

Mother and daughter were alone in the street under the mansion's lantern.

Sashenka knelt beside her mother, who was weeping. Her tears ran in black streams from black eyes on dirty white skin, like muddy footprints on old snow.

Sashenka pulled her to her feet, threw her arm over her shoulder and dragged her up the two steps into the lobby of the house. Inside, the great hall was almost dark, just an electric light burning on the first-floor landing. The giant white squares shone bright, while the black ones were like holes dropping to the middle of the earth. Somehow, she got her mother up to her room. The electric light would be too bright so she lit the oil lamps instead.

By now, Ariadna was sobbing quietly to herself. Sashenka raised her mother's hands to her lips and kissed them, her anger of a few moments earlier forgotten.

'Mama, Mama, you're home now. It's me, Sashenka! I'm going to undress you and put you to bed.' Ariadna calmed down a little, though she continued to speak slivers of nonsense as Sashenka undressed her.

'Sing it again . . . loneliness . . . your lips are like stars, houses . . . the wine is only mediocre, a bad year . . . hold me again . . . feel so sick . . . pay it, I'll pay, I can afford it . . . Love is God . . . am I home . . . you sound like my daughter . . . my vicious daughter . . . another glass please . . . kiss me properly.'

Sashenka pulled off her mother's boots, threw off the sable and the hat with ostrich feathers, unhooked the satin dress embroidered with sequins and misty with faded tuberose scent, untied the bodice, unrolled the shredded stockings, unclipped the brooches, the three ropes of pearls and the diamond earrings. As she pulled off the underdress and the lingerie that was inside out, she was enveloped in the animal smells and sweated alcohol of a woman of the town, aromas that repelled her. She vowed she would never let herself descend into such a state. Finally she heated water and washed her mother's face.

Amazed at herself, she realized that she had become the mother, and the mother the child. She folded and hung her mother's clothes, laid her jewels in the velvet box, threw her lingerie into the laundry basket. Then she helped her mother on to the bed, under the covers and kissed her cheek. She stroked her forehead and sat with her.

'You and me . . .' said Ariadna, as she fell asleep, rolling and tossing in her sad dreams.

'Sleep, Mama. There, there. It's over.'

'Darling Sashenka, you and me . . .'

When Ariadna finally slept, Sashenka wept. I don't want children, she told herself. Never!

CHAPTER 19

Sashenka was still asleep in the chair in Ariadna's boudoir when she heard her mother calling her: 'Sashenka! I'll take you shopping today, just as your father wanted. Chernyshev's for your day dresses! You might even be lucky enough to have a gown from Madame Brissac like the little Grand Duchesses!'

'But I've got to study,' said Sashenka, stretching, and going into her mother's bedroom.

'Don't be foolish, my dear,' said her mother cheerfully, as if nothing shocking had happened. 'Look at how you dress. Like a schoolteacher!'

Ariadna was having breakfast off a tray on her bed, and the room smelt of coffee, toast, caviar and poached eggs. 'We've become firm friends, haven't we, *sladkaya* – my sweetie?'

As Leonid finished serving and left the room, Ariadna winked at Sashenka, who asked herself how her mother could possibly have recovered so absolutely, so shamelessly, from the night's indulgences. The dissipated require constitutions of steel, she thought.

'I'm not sure I can come.'

'We leave at eleven. Lala's drawing you a bath.' Sashenka decided to acquiesce. Her days were interminably boring anyway. She lived for the dark hours.

An hour later, the two-tone coffee-hued Benz, the third family car, piloted by Pantameilion sporting what Sashenka privately called his 'bandmaster's garb', delivered them before the famous vitrines of mannequins in hats, toques and ball-dresses: the Chernyshev couture atelier on the corner of Greater Maritime and Nevsky.

The doors of the fashion emporium were opened by flunkeys in green frock coats. Inside, women wearing white gloves, hats like fruit bowls and tight-waisted dresses, pleated and whaleboned, tried on racks of dresses. The air was dense with perfume and the scent of warm bodies.

Ariadna commandeered the entire right side of the shop, much to Sashenka's embarrassment. A smiling fever of submissive enthusiasm attended Ariadna's every whim. At first Sashenka thought the staff were cringing like her at her mother's brashness but then she realized that the atmosphere reflected the jubilation felt in all luxury shops at the arrival of a very rich client with little taste and less restraint.

A stick insect in a red gown speaking poor French presided over this jamboree, barking orders. The assistants were almost too assiduous: weren't they smirking a little? Models (who, Sashenka thought, wore far too much foundation) walked up and down in dresses that did not interest her. Her mother pointed at this one or that one, in brocade or lace, with flounces or sequins, and even made her try on a couple. Lala, who accompanied mother and daughter, helped Sashenka into the dresses.

Sashenka had decided to enjoy the trip in order to avoid a row with her mother. But the dressing and undressing, the pulling and pushing, the staring and poking by the skinny non-Frenchwoman, who whipped pins in and out of the fabric with invisible speed, began to rile her. She hated the way she looked in every dress and found herself becoming angry and upset.

'I'm so ugly, Lala, in this. I refuse to wear it! I'd burn it!' Her mother, in her velvet skirt and fur-collar bolero jacket, was a gorgeous swan while Sashenka felt lumpier and fatter than a warthog. She could not bear to look in the mirrors again.

'But Mademoiselle Zeitlin has such a perfect figure for the latest fashions,' said the couturier. '*Quelle formidable poitrine!*'

'I hate myself in all this rubbish! I want to go home!'

'Poor Sashenka's tired, aren't you, darling?' Another wink. 'You don't have to have everything but there were some you liked, weren't there, sweetie?'

Feeling somewhat sheepish at this, Sashenka nodded.

A wave of relief now passed over the staff.

Glasses of Tokai were brought for Baroness Zeitlin, who threw her head back and laughed too loudly, paying in big green notes, and then the satisfied assistants helped the ladies rearrange their furs. Pantameilion followed them out of Chernyshev's, carrying their purchases in bulging bags which he quickly stowed in the boot.

'There!' said Ariadna, settling herself in the car. 'Now you have some grown-up dresses at last.'

'But Mama,' replied Sashenka, sickened by the expense and surprised such shops were still open in wartime, 'I don't lead that life. I just wanted something simple. I don't need balldresses and tea dresses and day dresses.'

'Oh yes you do,' answered Lala.

'I sometimes change six times in a day,' declared Ariadna. 'I wear a day dress in the morning. Then a tea dress and then today I'm going to call on the Lorises in my new chiffon dress with brocade, and then tonight . . .'

Sashenka could hardly bear to think of her mother at night.

'We women have got to make an effort to find husbands,' explained Ariadna.

'Where to, Baroness?' asked Pantameilion through the speaking tube.

'To the English Shop, Sashenka's favourite,' answered Ariadna.

Inside the shop, behind the windows that displayed Penhaligon's bath oils and scents, Pears soaps and Fortnum's Gentleman's Relish and

Cooper's jams, the women bought a ginger cake and biscuits while still lecturing Sashenka about the need for dresses.

'Hello, Sashenka! Is it you? Yes, it is!' Some young students in uniformed greatcoats and caps were lingering outside Chernyshev's, smirking and pushing against each other. 'Naughty Sashenka! We heard about your scrape with the gendarmes!' they called.

Sashenka noticed that the 'aesthetes' wore berets, the 'dandies' peaked caps. One of the aesthetes, who was heir to some magnate or other, had written her love poems. Sashenka smiled thinly and walked on ahead of her mother and Lala.

'Mademoiselle, what a pleasure to meet again!'

For a moment Sashenka froze, but then her senses returned as Captain Sagan walked briskly through the lurking students. He wore a tweed coat, a tartan tie and a Derby hat, all probably bought at the English Shop. He bowed, with a slight smile, raised the Derby and kissed her hand.

'I was buying some cufflinks,' he said. 'Why is everyone so keen on English style? Why not Scottish or Welsh or even Indian? They're our allies too.'

Sashenka shook her head and tried to remember what Mendel had ordered her to do. Her heart was thumping in the rhythm of a speeding train. This is it, Comrade Mendel! she told herself.

'I'm sure you never want to see me again, but there's Mayakovsky to discuss, and remember we never got to Akhmatova? I must rush. I hope I haven't . . . embarrassed you.'

'You've a hell of a nerve!' she exclaimed.

He raised his Derby, and she could not help but notice that he wore his hair long, more like an actor than a policeman.

Sagan waved at a waiting sleigh that slid forward with its bells ringing and carried him off down Nevsky.

Ariadna and Lala caught up with her.

'Sashenka!' said her mother. 'Who was that? You could have been a little more friendly.'

But Sashenka now felt invincible, however many silly dresses they had made her try on. She adored the secret nocturnal work of a Bolshevik activist. Now, she thought, I'll be a real asset to the Party. The house was watched. Sagan must have guessed that they would visit the English Shop, where he would stand out less than at Chernyshev's. He had spoken to her out of earshot of her mother and governess because he wanted her to know that he had his eye on her. She could not wait to tell Mendel.

On the way home, Ariadna squeezed her daughter's cheek.

'Sashenka and I are going to be firm friends, firm friends, aren't we, darling?' her mother kept saying.

Sitting on the tan leather between Ariadna and Lala, Sashenka remembered that in the past, whenever she had run to her mother for a cuddle, Ariadna had withdrawn from her, saying, 'Mrs

Lewis, Mrs Lewis, this is a new dress from Madame Brissac and the child's got a dirty mouth . . .'

Last night she had finally got her hug but now she no longer wanted it.

When they reached home, Ariadna took Sashenka's hand and coaxed her upstairs into her boudoir.

'Come out with me tonight in a new dress that shows off your figure!' she whispered huskily, sniffing the tuberose scent on her wrist. 'After last night, when I saw you coming home late, I know about your secret lover! I won't tell Papa but we can go out together. I thought you were such a prig, dear Sashenka, never smiling – no wonder you had no suitors – but I was wrong, wasn't I? Creeping home in the early hours like a pussycat! Who was the tomcat? That tweed suit and Derby we saw just now? We'll wear our gorgeous new gowns and people will think we're sisters. You and me, we're just the same . . .'

But Sashenka had to deliver a Party rubber stamp and the receipt book for contributions. At the safehouse, she would meet the comrades and boil the gelatine used to print the leaflets on the hectograph.

Before all those duties, she had to contact Mendel and tell him about her meeting with Sagan.

She longed for the mysteries of the night like the embrace of a lover.

CHAPTER 20

Sashenka left the house at 1am. Noting the two spooks on the street, she walked up to Nevsky Prospect and into the Europa Hotel. From the lobby she took the service lift down to the basement, walked through the kitchens, where bloody-aproned porters with shaggy beards were delivering eggs, cabbages and the pink carcasses of pigs and lambs, and out into the street again, where she hailed a troika and left a coded note for Mendel at the Georgian pharmacy on Alexandrovsky Prospect.

At the coachmen's café outside the Finland Station, she was eating a lukewarm pirozhki and listening to 'Yankee Doodle' on the barrel organ for the third time when a young man slipped into the seat opposite her. He was older, but they shared the grey fatigue of the night-dweller and the radiant conviction of the revolutionary.

'C-c-collect the b-b-bulldog from the comrade at the Horse Guards,' stuttered the student, who had little hazel eyes, thick steel-rimmed spectacles and a leather worker's cap on a peculiarly square head. This was Comrade Molotov, Sashenka realized, and he was twenty-six years old. He, Comrade Mendel and Comrade Shlyapnikov were the last Bolshevik leaders at liberty in the whole empire. When he took off his leather coat, he wore a short jacket and stiff collar like a clerk. Without his cap, his forehead bulged unnaturally. 'Ask for C-c-comrade Palitsyn. Anything to report?'

She shook her head.

'G-g-good luck, comrade.' Comrade Molotov was gone. Sashenka felt a thrill run down her spine.

At the Horse Guards, the concierge Verezin let her in again.

'What happened to the sable? And the Arctic fox?' he asked.

'Attracted too much attention,' she said. 'Is someone here for me?'

Comrade Ivan Palitsyn sat waiting beside some bottles at the round table by the stove. He stood up when she entered.

'I'm Comrade Vanya,' he said. 'I know you. I saw you talk to the workers' circle at the Putilov Works.' He offered a big red hand.

'I remember you,' she said. 'You were the only one who asked a question. I was very nervous.'

'No wonder,' said Vanya, 'a girl and an intellectual among us lot. You spoke passionately and we appreciated a girl like you coming to help us.'

Sashenka knew what he meant by 'a girl like you' and it touched a nerve. He must have noticed because he added gently, 'We come from such

136

different worlds, but you tell me what you know, and I'll share what I know.'

She was grateful. Shaggy-haired and six foot tall with the cheekbones and slanting eyes of his Tatar forefathers, Vanya Palitsyn personified the pure Russian brawn of peasant stock and the plain-spoken, practical fervour of the worker. She knew that, unlike Mendel or Molotov, he was the real thing, one who had toiled in the Putilov Works since he was eight, and he talked in the argot of a proletarian. This, thought Sashenka, is the hero for whom Marx had created his vision and for whom she had joined the movement.

'Comrade Snowfox, I've got something for you, several things in fact. You know what to do with them?'

'I do.'

'Sit. Do you want a drink of cognac or vodka? Me and Comrade Verezin are having a bit of a feast aren't we, Igor?'

'I've joined the Party,' said Verezin.

'Congratulations, Comrade Verezin,' said Sashenka. Only Party members deserved the respectful moniker 'comrade'. But Mendel had told her not to socialize, not to chatter. The intellectuals were much more paranoid than the real workers, she thought.

Vanya Palitsyn, who wore a fringed peasant blouse, boots and breeches, handed her the bulldog and a small package. The oiled metal of the pistol gleamed liquidly.

'Deliver this to the printer in the cellar bar on Gogol Street – he's a Georgian, a handsome devil. Don't lose your head!' Vanya looked her in the eye and smiled. 'The bulldog is for you.'

She walked past the Taurida Palace just after 3 am, and caught a tram down Liteiny. She felt the weight in her coat. The bulldog – a Mauser pistol – was in her pocket, fully loaded and with a spare cardboard box of ammunition. She ran her fingers over the weapon; the steel was freezing. For the first time, the Party had armed her. She had never fired a gun in earnest. Perhaps it was just one of Mendel's little tests? But what was revolution without dynamite? Did the Party need her to liquidate an agent provocateur? That set her thinking about Sagan. She knew he would find her again.

She hailed a one-horse sleigh to the Caravanserai bar on Gogol, a subterranean cavern with Turkish alcoves, used by poorer students, soldiers, some workers. The entrance was unremarkable but once inside she found that a passageway led under the street. She could smell cigarettes, sausages, stale wine, and felt a table of ragged students go quiet as she passed.

In a dark alcove on his own sat a man in a dashing Caucasian hood, white but lined with fur, and an army greatcoat. He raised a glass of red wine.

'I was waiting for you, Comrade Snowfox. I'm Hercules Satinov,' said the Georgian comrade, who had Russianized his real name of Satinadze. 'Follow me, comrade.'

He led her deeper into the bar, opening the door into a beer cellar. The air there was moist and fetid. Crouching, he lifted a manhole cover. Curling metal steps led down to the printing press. She could hear the deep rhythm of it turning over, like a mechanical bumble bee. Men in peasant smocks were bringing out piles of rough newspapers, which they bound up with red rope. The space reeked of oil and burnt paper.

Satinov pulled back his dashing white hood. 'I'm just back in Piter. From Baku.' His stiff, thick hair shone blue-black, growing low on his forehead. He was tall, wiry and muscular, and he radiated clean virile power. 'You have the newsprint for me?'

She handed over the package.

'Pleased to meet you, Comrade Snowfox,' he said without a hint of mockery, taking her hand and kissing it.

'Quite the Georgian knight!' she said a little defensively. 'Do you dance the *lezginka* too? Can you sing "*Suliko*"?'

'No one dances better than me. Perhaps we can sing some songs and drink some wine tonight?'

'No, comrade,' replied Sashenka. 'I've no time for such frivolities. Nor should you.'

Satinov did not seem to take offence. Instead he laughed loudly, raising his hands in surrender. 'Forgive me, comrade, but we Georgians aren't as cold-hearted as Russians! Good luck!' He led her to a different exit that emerged in a deserted courtyard behind Gogol Street.

At the end of the narrow alley, she checked her tail according to Mendel's training. No one. She waited. No one on the street at all. Suddenly she experienced a sort of dizzy jubilation: she wanted to laugh and dance gaily at the bleak glamour of these conspirators – Palitsyn at the Horse Guards, Satinov at the printer's, young men from different worlds but united in their determination. She knew in her heart that these characters were the future, her future. Her conviction made the dark roughness of this existence shine so bright. Small wonder that men like Mendel were addicted. Normality? Responsibility? Family, marriage, money? She thought of her father's delight at receiving his latest contract to supply 200,000 rifles, and her deluded, unhappy mother. That was death, she told herself, dreary, drab, living death.

She walked through an archway into another courtyard. This was one of Mendel's rules: try to avoid entering any building through the front door and always check there are two exits. In Russia, janitors and doormen lingered on the street and tended not to watch the courtyards.

Inside, she hurried to the rear door, opened it and sprang up the cold dark steps, using the half-light of the streetlamps to guide her to the top floor. She had been here earlier but her comrade had missed the rendezvous. Perhaps he would be here by now.

She unlocked the door, closing it behind her. The apartment was in darkness but it was sombre even

140

in daytime, a cavern of Asiatic rugs, old kerosene lamps, eiderdowns and mattresses. She inhaled the friendly aroma of mothballs, salted fish and yellowing books: an intellectual lived here. She went into the kitchen and tested the samovar as Mendel had taught her: it was cold. In the bedroom, the walls were covered in bookcases, *Apollo* and other intellectual journals in piles on the floor.

Yet something was not right. Her breath caught in her throat. Bristling with Bolshevik vigilance, she moved silently, nerves like forked lightning that jazzed down her spinal column. She turned into the sitting room. There was the rasp of a rough strike and a kerosene lamp sprang to life.

'Greetings! I thought you'd never come.' A familiar voice – so why did it give her such a shock?

'Don't mess with me,' she said, swallowing hard. She had the Mauser. 'Lift up the light.'

He illuminated his face. 'Did you buy some sweet dresses, Zemfira?'

Captain Sagan sat in the chair, wearing an ill-fitting black suit with a string tie. A fur coat lay on the floor.

'What are you doing here?' She was conscious that her voice sounded high and a little squeaky.

'Your comrade's not coming. We picked him up. Tomorrow, the Special Commission'll sentence him to two years of Siberian exile. Nothing too serious. So rather than leave you to waste your evening, I came instead.'

She shrugged, struggling to remain calm. 'So?

This safehouse will no longer be safe. If you're not arresting me, I'll go home and get some sleep. Goodnight.' As she turned, she remembered Mendel's order. She needed to get to know Sagan better. Besides, she was curious as to why he was here. 'Or perhaps it's too late for sleep?'

'I think so,' he said, pushing back his hair and looking younger suddenly. 'Are you a night owl?'

'I feel lazy in the mornings but I come to life at night. All this conspiracy suits me. What about you, Captain? If I'm a night owl, you're a bat.'

'I live on a knife-edge. Like you and your uncle Mendel. I sleep so little that when I go home to bed, I find I can hardly settle. I get up and read poems. This is what happens to us. We enjoy it so much that it changes us and we can't do anything else. We conspirators, Sashenka, are like the undead. The vampires. We feed on the blood of the workers, and you feed on the blood of the bloodsuckers themselves who suck the blood of the workers. Quite Darwinian.'

She laughed aloud and sat on the edge of a metal bed, where the mattress was dyed sepia yellow by the hissing lamp.

'We conspirators? There's no parallel between us, you police pharaoh. We have a scientific programme; you're simply reacting to us. We'll win in the end. You'll be finished. You're digging the grave of the exploiters for us.'

Captain Sagan chuckled. 'Yet I see no sign of this. At the moment, your vaunted Party is just a few freaks: the intellectual Mendel Barmakid, a worker named Shlyapnikov, a middle-class boy named Scriabin (Party alias Molotov), a few workers' circles, some troublemakers at the front. Lenin's abroad, and the rest are in Siberia. That leaves you, Sashenka. There can't be more than a thousand experienced Bolsheviks in the whole of Russia. But you're having a lot of fun, aren't you? Playing the revolutionary.'

'You're deluding yourself, Sagan,' she said hotly. 'The queues are growing longer, the people getting angrier, hungrier. They want peace and you're asking them to die for Nicholas the Last, Nicholas the Bloody, the German traitor Alexandra and the pervert Rasputin . . .'

'Whom you know all about from your mother. Let me try some thoughts on you. Your parents are the very definition of the corruption of the Russian system.'

'Agreed.'

'The aspirations and rights of the workers and peasants are totally ignored by the present system.'

'True.'

'And we know that the peasants need food but they also need rights and representation, and protection from the capitalists. They must have land, and they are desperate for peace. Your father's dream of a progressive group taking power is too little, too late. We need a real change.'

'Since we agree on everything, why aren't you a Bolshevik?'

'Because I believe a revolution could come soon.'

'So do I,' said Sashenka.

'No, you don't. As a Marxist, you know a socialist revolution isn't yet possible. The Russian proletariat isn't yet developed. That's where we differ. According to you, there'll be no Bolshevik revolution.'

Sashenka sighed. 'Our beliefs are so close. It's a shame we don't agree on that.'

They were silent for a moment then Sagan changed the subject. 'You've heard the new Mayakovsky?'

'Can you recite it?'

'Let me try:

'To you who lived from orgy to orgy
To you who love only wine and food . . .'

Sashenka took it up:

'Why should I give my life for your convenience?
I'd be better off serving pineapple water
To the whore at the bar.'

'Beautifully declaimed, Mademoiselle Zeitlin. I salute you!'

'In our country, poetry's more powerful than howitzers.'

'You're right. We should use poetry more and the gallows less.'

She watched him closely, keenly aware that both

of them were risking their lives in what Mendel called the Superlative Game.

Her hand was on the frozen butt of the Mauser. A few weeks previously, Mendel had arranged for her to be taken out of the city to the birch forests and taught how to shoot: soon she could hit the target more than she missed it. When the Party ordered her to kill Sagan, she would do so.

'What are you carrying?'

The gun at her fingertips made her heart thump. She heard her voice and it did not sound like hers any more. It was stranger, deeper, surprisingly calm. 'Arrest me if you wish. Then you can have some Medusa of a policewoman search me.'

'There's only one big difference between us, Sashenka. I believe human life is sacred. You believe in terror. Why do your comrades have to kill? I wonder if there is something in their mentality that suits them to this creed? Are they criminals or madmen?'

She stood up again. 'Do you have a home to go to, Captain? Are you married?'

'Yes.'

'Children?'

'Not yet.'

'Happy?' Sashenka rubbed her eyes, now weary.

'Are any marriages happy?' he answered.

'I pity you,' she said. 'I'll never marry. Goodnight.'

'One thing, Zemfira: do you think there's anywhere I'd rather be than here?'

Sashenka frowned. 'That's no compliment. I suspect most men don't want to go home. Particularly when they're vampires like you and me.' We are both armed, she thought almost deliriously. We could both die tonight.

Outside again, Sashenka walked through the streets with a light sleet caressing her face and eyelashes. Sagan was certainly an odd sort of gendarme, she reflected. She was playing along with him, drawing him out. He was older than her, much older, and he had recruited many double agents but his smug confidence in his gamesmanship was his Achilles heel. Somehow, she'd break him down and deliver him to the Party, like John the Baptist's head on a platter.

Far away, a train rushed whistling through the night. The black smoke of the factories encircled a silver moon. It was almost dawn: the sky was tinged with pink; the snow a deep purple. The muffled trot of a sleigh approached, and she hailed it.

The bulldog was so cold in her pocket, it burned her fingers.

'The price of oats is up again,' said the coachman, pulling on his tangled beard as they trotted towards the Zeitlin house on Greater Maritime Street.

CHAPTER 21

Zeitlin knocked on the door of Ariadna's boudoir and entered without waiting for an answer. It was midday but she was still in bed, wearing a silk nightgown with blue bows that revealed the bruised white skin of her shoulders. The room smelt of coffee and tuberose. Leonid had brought her breakfast earlier, and the painted wooden tray with its dirty plates and empty glasses now stood on a stand beside the bed. Luda the maid was laying out the dresses for that day – one for a luncheon, one for calling on friends, one for drinks, then one for a dinner. Four outfits, Zeitlin noted. Were so many dresses really necessary?

'Will this do for tea, Baroness?' Luda appeared from the boudoir holding up a crêpe-de-Chine dress. 'Oh Baron! Good morning.' She bowed.

'Leave us alone, Luda.'

'Yes, Baron.'

'Sit down, Samuil,' said Ariadna, stretching. She was enjoying letting him see her flesh, he could tell. 'What is it? Has the Bourse crashed? That's all you care about, isn't it?'

'I'll stand.' He was conscious that he was clenching his cigar between his teeth.

She stiffened. 'What's happened? You always sit down. Shall I send for coffee?' She reached for the bell but was distracted by the smoothness of her upper arm, which she nuzzled against her lips.

'No, thank you.'

'Please yourself. I had such fun last night. I saw the Elder again. He told me such fascinating things, Samuil. Everyone was talking about the new Premier. Samuil?'

'I want a divorce, Ariadna.' There – he'd said it.

There was a long silence, then Zeitlin saw the words register. She shook her head, and raised a hand as if trying to speak.

'You? But why? We've lived like this for years. You're not a jealous man. You're too . . . too confident for that. You're joking surely, Samuil. We've been married for eighteen years. Why now?'

Zeitlin took a puff of his cigar, trying to appear calm and rational.

'It's just . . . weariness.'

'Weariness? You're divorcing me out of weariness?'

'You'll have a generous allowance. Nothing will change. You'll just be living in a different house. Is it such a shock?'

'You can't!' He had turned to leave but she jumped out of bed and threw herself to the floor at his feet, knocking the cigar out of his hands. He bent to catch it and she gripped him so hard that he lost his balance and fell beside her. She'd begun to weep, her eyes wild, the whites rolling. He tried to release himself but, in the process, tore her nightgown, exposing her breasts. Yet still she held on to him so hard that the diamond studs on his stiff shirtfront popped out on to the floor.

They lay side by side, breathing heavily. He looked down and noticed her long dark-brown nipples peering through her thick tresses. She looked like a gypsy dancer. This is how her lovers must see her, he thought, marvelling at her uninhibited wantonness. How strange are we humans, he reflected. The light is dark, the night is bright.

Over the years, while they were strangers by day, they had still shared a passion by night. In daylight she either worried or disgusted him, but then she would come to him in the early hours, her breath stale with old champagne, fresh brandy and yesterday's scent, other men's cigars, and whisper to him of adventures of startling depravity. She hissed an argot of peasant Polish and gutter Yiddish, the language they had spoken when they first met at the court of her father, the Turbin rabbi, in that Jewish village near Lublin.

What things she told him, what delicious visions! Desires and exploits almost incredible for a respectable lady! One night a lover had taken her to the Summer Gardens, a place of dogs and prostitutes . . . she spared him no detail. Roused to a fever, he performed erotic feats worthy of an athlete, he the most moderate of men who regarded passion as a dangerous thing. But in the morning he awoke feeling filthy and remorseful, as if he had met a whore in a seedy room and made a fool of himself. And this was his own wife!

'Aren't I still beautiful?' she asked him, smelling of tuberose and almonds. 'How can you leave *this*? You can make love to me. Go on, push me down. You know you want to. But you're so cold. No wonder I've been so unhappy. You're joking about the divorce, aren't you? Samuil?' She began to laugh, almost to herself, but then she threw back her head, laughing huskily from her belly. He could feel the warmth radiating from her skin like heat from a burning coal, could smell the taint of her excitement. She took his hand and plunged it between her thighs, then pointed at the mirror. 'Look at us! Look at us, Samoilo! What a good-looking pair! Like when we met. Remember? You said you'd never met a girl like me. What did you say? "You're like wild horses."'

Samuil had meant it differently – he had wondered even then if she was too unpredictable to marry.

He stood up, not without difficulty, adjusting his clothes. 'Ariadna, we've become ridiculous.'

The servants had talked: Pantameilion had told Leonid, who had agonized how to tell the master that Sashenka had rescued her mother, drunk in the street. The butler had despatched Shifra, Zeitlin's own ancient governess, to tell him this unpalatable news. Zeitlin had not reacted, simply thanking Shifra politely, kissing her blue-veined hand and showing her to the door again. Historians, thought Zeitlin, try to find a single explanation for events but really things happen for many reasons, not one. Lighting up his Montecristo cigar, he reflected on Sashenka's arrest, on Mrs Lewis's belief that he barely knew his own daughter – and on the unwelcome arrival of Rasputin in his life (which was somehow worse than Ariadna's lovers). While his irrepressible brother Gideon sought his pleasures recklessly because 'I might croak at any minute and go straight to hell,' Zeitlin had believed that calm discipline would ensure a long life.

Then last night he had been visited by dreams of sudden death, train crashes, gunshots, smashed automobiles, the house on fire, overturned sleighs, revolution, blood on the snow, himself on a deathbed dying of consumption of the intestines and angina pectoris, with Sashenka weeping beside him – and at the very gates of heaven, he had realized he was carrying nothing. He'd invested in treasure, not love. He was naked and he had wasted his life.

At dawn, he had gone to Shifra in the pantry – but the old witch, crouched in the chair like a translucent spider, already knew his dreams. 'You need love in your life too,' she'd told him. 'Don't always live for the future. There might not be a future. Who knows what's written for you in the Book of Life?'

Zeitlin hated change and feared shaking the foundations of his world. But something in the Chain of Being was shifting and he could not help himself. Against his better judgement, in a trance that he believed might be the presence of Fate, he'd gone to Ariadna's room.

Now he looked down at his wife, still lying in a tangle of easy limbs on the floor.

'Is there someone else?' she asked. 'Are you in love with some ballerina from the Mariinsky? A gypsy bitch from the Bear? If there is, I don't care. You see, you selfish, cold fool, I just don't care! I'm going to be as good as a nun. The Elder is showing me the rosy path to redemption. We have another appointment next week, on 16 December. Just Rasputin and me. 'I will teach you, Honey Bee,' he says. 'You've sinned so much, you ooze Satan's darkness. Now I'll teach you love and redemption.' That was what he told his Honey Bee. He's kind to me. He listens to me for hours on end even when his antechamber is filled with petitioners, generals, countesses . . .'

Zeitlin clicked his studs on to his shirt and retied his cravat.

'I just want to live a normal life,' he said quietly. 'I'm not so young and I might drop dead at any minute. Is that so strange? Flek will arrange everything.' And feeling a quiet sorrow and fear of the future, he left closing the door behind him.

CHAPTER 22

On the broad glowing screen of the Piccadilly Cinema on Nevsky, the matinee that afternoon was entitled *Her Heart Is a Toy in His Hands*. Sashenka was late and missed the beginning but as she raised her face to the screen and lit up a cigarette, she soon gathered that the gentleman in question was a supposedly handsome dandy (who actually looked like a stuffed dummy) wearing tails and white tie on a beach while the lady in a red-tinted balldress stared out at a sea of blue-tinted waves.

On stage a quartet of students from the Conservatoire were playing music chosen to represent the sea breeze. The lady's heart had been toyed with enough, and she'd begun to wade into the ocean. A fat man in a tailcoat ran on to the stage and started to turn a wheel on a brass machine. The quartet ceased playing and the machine produced a sound that resembled the crunch and swish of the surf.

In the darkness of the half-full Piccadilly, the air was dry with electricity, and silvery cigarette smoke curled through the beam of light that projected the images. A peasant soldier sitting with his sweetheart commented loudly: 'She's in the water! She's stepping into the sea.' A couple in the back were kissing passionately, both probably married and too poor to afford a hotel. A drunk snored. But most stared at the images in rapt amazement. Sashenka had just delivered a message from Mendel to Satinov, the Georgian comrade who wore the hood, and she had an hour to kill before meeting Comrade Vanya over in Vyborg. Then it was home for supper as usual. *The End* declared the ornate letters on a black background before a new picture show was announced: *The Skin of Her Throat Was Alabaster*.

Sashenka sighed loudly.

'You think it's nonsense?' said a voice beside her. 'Where's your sense of romance?'

'Romance? You're the smiling cynic,' she said. It was Sagan. 'You realize that we'll conquer Russia with the silver screen? We will paint the world red. I thought you slept during the day?'

Since Sashenka's arrest, they had been meeting every two or three days, sometimes in the middle of the night. She reported to Mendel on every detail. 'Be patient,' he said. 'Keep playing. One day, he'll offer something.'

'He thinks he can flatter me as a fellow intellectual.'

'Let him. Even the Okhrana are human and will make human mistakes. Make him like you.'

She never knew when she would see the secret

policeman. In between discussions about poetry, novels and ideology, he had asked questions about the Party – was Mendel still in the city? Who was the new Caucasian comrade? Where did Molotov live? And she responded by asking, as specified by Mendel, what raids were planned, what arrests, was there a double agent in the committee?

On the screen the new moving picture had started. The quartet played a sweeping melody on their strings.

'I'm not here for the film,' said Captain Sagan, suddenly serious. 'I've got a troika waiting outside. You need to come with me.'

'Why should I? Are you arresting me again?'

'No, your mother's in trouble. I'm doing you and your family a favour. I'll explain on the way.'

They climbed into the troika, pulled the bear-rug over their laps, and sat swathed in furs as the sleigh skated over the ice with that effervescent swish that felt like flight. The streets were already dark but the electric lights were shining. Low Finnish sledges decorated with ribbons and jingling bells and screaming students rushed through the streets, their silhouettes forming cut-outs against the snow. The food shortages were spreading, prices rising, and Sashenka spotted a massive queue of working women jostling outside a bakery. The worse, the better, she thought glee-fully. The sirens of the Vyborg factories whistled. The snow, so rarely white, glowed a gritty orange.

'Are you taking me home?'

Sagan shook his head. 'To Rasputin's place. He's disappeared. Dead, I think.'

'So? That's a shame for us: he's won us more recruits than the *Communist Manifesto*.'

'On that, Zemfira, we differ. For us, it's a blessing from heaven. The body's under the ice somewhere – we'll find him. The Empress is distraught. He never came home from a party at the Yusupov Palace. Young Felix, the transvestite Prince Yusupov, is up to his neck in it but he's married to a Grand Duchess.'

'And my mother?'

'Your mother was waiting for Rasputin at his apartment. I thought, after the other night, you'd be the one to help . . .'

Police in grey uniforms with lambskin collars guarded the doorway of 64 Gorokhovaya Street. Shabby young men in student overcoats with note-books and unwieldy cameras tried to talk their way past the barriers but Sashenka and Captain Sagan were let straight through.

In the courtyard, gendarmes in their handsome dark blue uniforms with silver buttons sheltered from the cold. Sashenka noticed that even though Sagan was in plain clothes, they saluted him.

At the top of the stairs, the stiff shirts, well-cut suits and smart two-tone shoes marked out the urbane Okhrana officers from the grizzled beards, red noses and grubby shoes of the police detect-ives handling the murder investigation. The

Okhrana officers greeted Sagan and updated him in coded jargon that reminded Sashenka of the Bolsheviks. Perhaps all secret organizations are the same, she thought.

'Come to collect her mother,' Sagan told his colleagues, taking her wrist. She decided not to withdraw it.

'Go on up – but hurry,' his Okhrana colleague told him. 'The Director's on his way over. The minister's been reporting to Her Imperial Majesty at Tsarskoe Selo but he'll be here soon.'

As they neared the apartment, Sashenka could hear the sound of howling. It was raucously uninhibited in the way that peasants grieved. She thought of the air-raid sirens and then a dog she once saw, its legs sliced off by a car. She entered a lobby; to the left, the steamy kitchen with the samovar; a table spread with silks and furs; and then right, into the main sitting room, in the middle of which was a table with a half-drunk glass of the Elder's Madeira. The place smelt to Sashenka exactly like the huts of the peasants on the Zeitlin estates in Ukraine but, among the soupy cabbagey smells, there was just a hint of Parisian scent. Nothing in the place quite fitted, she thought: it was a peasant *izba* crossed with a government office and a bourgeois family home. It was like the hideout of a gypsy gang of robbers.

There was a sudden flurry of activity behind them and a general of the gendarmes, surrounded by an entourage, entered the main room.

Sagan hurried out, saluted, conferred and returned. 'They've found the body. In the Neva. It's him.' He crossed himself, then raised his voice. 'All right. We've got to get her home now. She's been here since last night.'

The howling grew louder and more shrill. Sagan opened the double doors into a small dark room with scarlet rugs and pillows and a large divan.

The shrieking was so animalistic, the shapes within the room so hard to identify that Sashenka stepped back, but Sagan caught her around the waist and again took her hand. She was grateful but most of all shocked. Bloody spots danced before her as her eyes adjusted to the gloom and she was able to see.

'She's in there. I have a car waiting for you downstairs but she should go before the press get in here. Go on. Don't be afraid,' Sagan said gently. 'It's just noise.'

She stepped inside.

It was hard at first to see how the bodies and limbs fitted together. Some women, arms around one another, crouched on the floor, rocking together, sobbing hysterically and ululating like Asiatics. Among them Sashenka saw her mother, her head shaking convulsively, her features hollow, her mouth a gash of scarlet screaming.

'Where am I?' cried her mother, her voice high and rough from wailing. 'Who are you?'

The air inside was a broth of raw sweat and

158

expensive scents. Sashenka knelt down and tried to reach Ariadna but her mother rolled away.

'No! No! Where's Grigory? He's coming, I know it.'

Sashenka, now on both knees, tried to get a hold of her mother but this time Ariadna slipped through her fingers, with a manic laugh. A fat woman on all fours began to bellow. Sashenka had a sudden urge to get up and run away, yet this was her own mother and she now realized, if she had never grasped it before, that Ariadna was not just a bad mother, she was sick, almost demented. A tall, black-haired ox of a young peasant, with black hair on her upper lip and eyebrows that grew together, seized Sashenka, shouting curses. Sashenka fought back but her attacker, whose mouth was edged with a white paste, sank her teeth into her arm. Sashenka shouted in pain, tossing aside this peasant woman, who Sagan later told her was Rasputin's daughter, and reached for her mother in earnest. She took her arm and then her leg and dragged her out of the fray. The other women tried to stop her but Sagan and an ordinary policeman pushed them back.

The creature who had been her mother lay at her feet, shivering and sobbing, under the cool eyes of Sagan and the policemen, who were discussing the post mortem on Rasputin's body and who might have murdered him. There was a pain in her forearm: Sashenka could see the individual toothmarks of her assailant. She noticed that Ariadna wore a simple floral dress quite unlike anything she had seen her wear before, and understood that she had intended to come before the Elder Grigory as a poor supplicant.

Sashenka fell to her knees, her hands clasped. She wanted to cry too. Sagan's hand came to rest on her shoulder.

'Pull yourself together, Mademoiselle Zeitlin. You've got to get her out of here *now*,' said Sagan, donning his Derby hat. 'I'll help you.'

Sashenka and Sagan took Ariadna by the arms and dragged her to the door.

On the landing, Ariadna started screaming again. 'Grigory, Grigory, where are you? We need you to soothe our souls and forgive our sins! Grigory! I've got to wait for him! He'll come back for me . . .' She struggled out of their hands, scratching and kicking, and tried to bolt back into the apartment but, moving fast, Sagan caught her.

'Gentlemen, we could do with a hand!' he called to the two city policemen guarding the door. One of them took Sashenka's place on Ariadna's left arm; Sagan took the right. The other policeman pulled down his hat, and in a fluid motion swept up Ariadna's two feet in his arms. The three of them carried Ariadna down the stairs, her dress riding up to reveal the shreds of her stockings and her bare legs.

Sashenka averted her gaze and walked ahead of them, horrified and helpless yet grateful for their assistance. She crossed the courtyard, feeling the eyes of the policemen on her, hoping they would not know that this mess was her mother. Pity and shame engulfed her.

A car with a gendarme sergeant at the wheel was backing through the archway into the courtyard.

'Get her inside,' said Sagan breathlessly. Another gendarme opened the back door and helped guide Ariadna into the compartment. 'Take her home, Sashenka.' Sagan slammed the door. 'Good luck.' He leaned in towards the driver. 'Thank you, Sergeant. Greater Maritime Street and fast!' Sagan banged the roof of the car.

Sashenka was alone in the compartment with her mother – and it took her back in time to the years after the revolution of 1905. She could just remember the Cossack horsemen and the furious shabby crowds and how Zeitlin had sent them out of Russia, to the west. They had travelled through Europe in a private railway carriage. Ariadna, always soused even then, wore scarlet brocade and held court at the Grand Hotel Pupp in Carlsbad, the Carlton in Nice, Claridge's in London, always accompanied by some new 'uncle'. There was the pink-cheeked Englishman, a Guards officer with a gold breastplate and a bearskin hat; a nimble Spanish diplomat in a frock coat; and Baron Mandro (known to Sashenka as 'the Lizard'), an ageing Galician Jew with an eyepatch, rouged cheeks and hairy hands like cockroaches, who had once patted her bottom. When she bit him – she could still taste his coppery blood on her tongue – Ariadna had slapped her. 'Get her out of here, vicious child!' and Sashenka was carried out of the room, struggling and screaming. And now, a decade later, Ariadna was being carried out, kicking and howling.

Sashenka peered out of the window. She longed to be in the streets, factories and safehouses with her comrades, away from this domestic farrago. The restaurants and nightclubs were filled with people. Whores trooped past St Isaac's towards the Astoria dressed in so much scarlet, gold and shining leather that through the snow and darkness Sashenka thought they resembled a regiment of Chevalier Guards. St Petersburg was in a fever. Never had the stakes in the poker games been so high, never had there been so many revellers, so many limousines outside the Astoria . . . Was it the last mazurka?

As Ariadna's head fell on to her daughter's shoulder, Sashenka told herself she was a Marxist and a Bolshevik, and she had nothing to do with her parents any more.

CHAPTER 23

'Your guest is already here, *mon baron*.'

Zeitlin had asked a woman to meet him at the Donan at 24 Moika. At night the restaurant was crowded with ministers, nabobs, courtesans, profiteers and probably spies but during the day they held court in the foyer and café of the Europa Hotel. In the afternoon the Donan was deserted, which was why Zeitlin often used its private rooms to hold discreet meetings: it was here in his usual private dining room, known as the baron's *kabinet*, that he had met the War Minister in August 1914 to clinch the deal to supply the army with rifle butts.

That morning he had called Jean-Antoine, the maître-d'. Born in Marseilles, Jean-Antoine was celebrated for his discretion, his ability to recall everyone he had ever met, and his tact in resolving the most outrageous scenes.

'*Mais d'accord, mon baron*,' Jean-Antoine replied. 'Your *kabinet*'s ready. Champagne on ice? Your favourite crayfish? Or just English tea, English cakes and Scotch whisky?'

'Just the tea.'

'I'll send over to the English Shop right away.'

Zeitlin usually took the automobile but that afternoon he had donned his *shapka* hat with earmuffs, his black coat with the beaver collar and his *valenki* galoshes over his patent-leather grey shoes (from Lobb's of London) and picked up his cane with the silver wolf's head – and he had let himself out of his house without ringing the bell.

Zeitlin relished the anonymity of moving through the dark streets without chauffeur or footman. It was not snowing but the ice was grinding into an adamantine freeze all over again. He could almost hear the grey glaze of the Neva River fusing together its fractures and fissures. In the streets, the gas lamps were being lit, the trams clattering over their rails. Behind him, bells and laughter pealed. A sleigh bearing students crammed together and holding on for dear life slid past him and was gone. These days, youngsters did what the hell they liked, Zeitlin thought. They had no values, no discipline.

Was he happier now that he was rich? Look at his crazy wife! And there was his darling Sashenka, a riddle to her own father. He loved her and longed to protect her. Yet she no longer seemed interested in her own family. She was almost a stranger, and sometimes he thought she despised him.

He wished he could weep as freely as a child. Like an old man singing his school song, he found himself humming the Kol Nidre tune from his childhood, which told of a vanishing world. He had hated it then but now he wondered: what if it was the right way?

He popped into Yegorov's, the bathhouse with its Gothic mahogany walls and stained-glass windows, and a page in white tunic and black breeches showed him to a cubicle. Stripping naked, he entered the icy bath and slipped under the iron bridge, draped in lush foliage, that arched over the water. Then he steamed for a while on a granite table. Several naked men, their bald heads and buttocks oddly alike in their pinkness and shininess, were being beaten with birch twigs. Zeitlin lay there ignoring everyone and thinking.

I'd pray to God if I was sure there was one, he told himself, but if he exists, we are just worms in the dust to him. Success is my religion. I make my own history.

Yet in his heart Zeitlin believed there was something out there greater than mankind. Behind his cigar smoke, studded shirt, frock coat, striped English trousers and spats, he was still a Jew, a believer in God in spite of himself. He had studied at the cheder, learning the Shulhan Aruk, the rules of living, the Pentateuch, the five books of the Bible that formed the Torah, the Jewish law, and the pedantic, wise, archaic poetry of the Talmud and the Mishnah.

After about an hour he dressed, splashing on his cologne, and walked back to Nevsky. The tall, glassy effulgence of the Fabergé shop glinted out of the darkness.

'Good evening, *barin*! Jump in, I'll give you a ride!' called out a Finnish sledge-driver, flicking his whip and slowing his stumpy-legged ponies, their jingling bells ringing festively.

Zeitlin waved the sledge-driver away and walked on with a spring in his step. I have been safe but captive for decades, he thought. I'm returning to life after a long hibernation. I am going to reclaim my daughter, show her how I love her, interest myself in her tutoring and her further studies. It is never too late, never too late, is it?

At the Donan, Jean-Antoine greeted him. Zeitlin threw off his coat and hat and kicked off his galoshes. He was looking forward to greeting his guest.

Inside the scarlet womb of his private *kabinet*, Lala awaited him in a prim shantung tea dress decorated with mauve flowers. She stood up when he came in, her gentle heart-shaped face quizzical.

'Baron! What's so urgent?'

'Don't say anything,' he said, taking her hands in his. 'Let's sit down.'

'Why here?'

'I'll explain.'

There was a knock on the door, and waiters brought in the tea: fruit cake, muffins with strawberry jam, fresh cream and two thimble glasses of amber. Lala stood up to serve, but he stopped her and waited until the waiters had poured the tea and closed the door.

'A brandy,' he said. 'For both of us.'

'What is it?' she asked. 'You're worrying me. You don't seem yourself. And why the cognac?'

'It's the best. Courvoisier. Try it.'

They eyed one another anxiously. Zeitlin knew he looked old, that his face was lined, that there were new fingers of grey at his temples. He was exhausted by relentless meetings and his own bonhomie, desiccated by columns of figures. Everyone expected so much of him, his obligations seemed unending. Even the profits of his own companies ground him down.

Lala seemed older too, he thought suddenly. Her cheeks were plumper and coarser, with red veins, the skin weathered by the winters, and there were crow's feet around her eyes. Fear of the future and of solitude, secret disappointments, had aged her.

Ashamed of these thoughts, he hesitated as the little wood fire surged up, dyeing their faces orange. She sipped the cognac. Slowly the fire warmed them.

She stood up. 'I don't like the cognac. It burns my throat. I think I should go. I don't like the feel of this place. It's not respectable . . .'

'This is the Donan!'

'Quite,' she said. 'I've read about it in the newspapers . . .'

It was no good. He could restrain himself no longer. He threw himself at her feet and buried his face in her lap, his tears wetting her shantung dress.

'What's wrong? For heaven's sake, what is it?'

He took her hands. She tried to push him away but somehow the kindness that was so much a part of her overcame her habit of prudence. Gently, she stroked his hair, and he could feel her hands soft and warm like a girl's.

He stood up and took her in his arms.

What am I doing? he thought. Have I gone mad? My God, the lips have their own rules. Just as magnesium burns on contact with oxygen, so skin on skin unleashes some sort of chemical reaction. He kissed her.

She sighed quietly under her breath. He knew she was an inveterate giver of affection – but didn't she want some for herself too?

Then something magical happened. He kissed her again and suddenly she kissed him back, eyes closed. His hands ran over her body. The very plainness of her dress, the cheapness of her stockings, the ordinariness of her rosewater scent delighted him. When he touched higher, he could barely conceive of the silkiness of her thigh. The smell of soap on skin, the smoke from the fire, the steaming tang of the India tea, entranced them both.

I am doing something utterly reckless, out of character and foolish, Zeitlin told himself. I who have control over everything I do. Stop right now, you fool. Don't be like your absurd brother! I'll be a laughing stock! I'll shatter my perfect world.

But it was already shattered, and Zeitlin found he did not care.

CHAPTER 24

At fourteen, Audrey Lewis had left the village school in Pegsdon, Hertfordshire, to take a job as junior nanny with the family of Lord Stisted in Eaton Square, London. Her story, as she herself said later, was as sadly predictable as one of the cheap novels she enjoyed reading. Seduction and impregnation by the feckless son of the house (who specialized in servant girls), and her subsequent arranged marriage to Mr Lewis, the fifty-year-old chauffeur, 'so as not to frighten the horses'. Her abortion was humiliating, painful and she almost died from a haemorrhage; the marriage did not prosper, and she left her position with the bribe of a glowing reference. Her adoring parents begged her to come home to their pub – The Live and Let Live in Pegsdon, which they had named to reflect their philosophy of life. But then she saw the advertisement in the *Lady*. One word was enough for her: Russia!

It was high summer in St Petersburg when the Zeitlin carriage met the young English girl as she disembarked from the German liner. Samuil wore a white suit, spats, a boater, an opal ring, a snake-shaped silver tiepin and an air of generous optimism that immediately included Audrey in his family's happiness. He was slim and young with his auburn hair and boulevardier's moustache. The Zeitlins did not yet live in the mansion on Greater Maritime but in a spacious apartment on Gorokhovaya. They were rich but still provincial: Ariadna, with her violet eyes, her blue-black hair and her queenly bust, remained the girl who had dazzled the private boxes at the theatres in the southern cities where her husband conducted his business. Ariadna was still busy keeping up with those snobbish provincials, the wives of the Russian viceroys and officers, and the Armenian and Muslim oil barons in Baku and Tiflis.

The Zeitlins, Lala discovered, were Jews. She had never met Jews before. There were no Jews in her village in Hertfordshire and Lord Stisted knew no Jews, although Lady Stisted talked disdainfully of the unscrupulous Jewish diamond millionaires from South Africa and the thousands of filthy Jewish cutthroats from Russia who had turned the East End into a 'rookery of crime'. Audrey had been warned that Jews were not good people to work for – but she knew her own position would not stand too much scrutiny. The Zeitlins for their part were delighted to find a girl who had worked in a noble London household. They suited each other – especially as the Zeitlins seemed very civilized Israelites.

The moment Lala arrived, indeed before her cases had been taken to her room, Ariadna, who looked dazzling in a dress of turquoise crépe de Chine, led her into a nursery to meet her charge.

'Here she is! *Voilà ma fille*,' said Ariadna in her pretentious Franco-English. 'She almost killed me when she was born. Never again. I've told Samuil – from now on, I deserve some fun! She's an unbiddable child, ungrateful and unruly. See if you can tame her a little, Mrs Linton—'

'Lewis, Audrey Lewis, madame.'

'Yes, yes . . . from now on, she's yours.'

It was at that meeting that Mrs Lewis had become Lala, and had fallen in love with Sashenka. She herself was in her teens; this child not that much younger. Her doctor in London had told her after the abortion that she would never have a child of her own and suddenly, passionately, she wanted to nurture this young girl.

The child and her governess needed each other and so Lala became Sashenka's mother, her *real* mother. What fun they had: skating and sleigh rides in winter, carriage rides, mushroom collecting and blackberry picking at Zemblishino in the summer, always laughing and always together.

The Zeitlins travelled constantly, to Odessa and Baku and Tiflis, by train but in a private compartment. Lala studied Russian on the long trips.

In Baku they stayed in a palace that Zeitlin's father had had copied from a French chateau: they promenaded on the seafront surrounded by a phalanx of *kochis*, armed bodyguards sporting fezes, wielding Berdana rifles. In Odessa they stayed at the Londonskaya Hotel right on Seaside Street, just above the famous Richelieu Steps: Lala spent her free time sitting in cafes, eating sturgeon kebabs on Deribaskaya. But her English heart remained in Tiflis.

Spring was a glory in Tiflis, magical Tiflis in Georgia, Tiflis the capital of the Caucasus, midway between the Zeitlin oil wells in Baku, on the Caspian Sea, and the Zeitlin oil tankers in Batum, on the Black Sea.

There the Zeitlins rented the mansion of a penniless Georgian prince, on a cobbled lane nestled into the steep slopes of Holy Mountain. Russian colonels and Armenian millionaires called at the house. Ariadna greeted them, laughing under her breath, from among the vines on the balcony, her hungry white teeth and violet eyes glistening. She never visited the nursery.

'Lewis and child are coming with the baggage' was her line. But even though he was so busy, Zeitlin would drop in on the nursery. He seemed to prefer it to Ariadna's 'at homes' full of officers and bureaucrats in frock coats and top hats, sashes and shoulderboards. In the highest circles, children were to be admired briefly and then removed from sight, but Zeitlin adored his Sashenka and kissed her forehead again and again.

'I must go back to work,' he'd say. 'But you're so sweet, darling Sashenka. Your skin is like rich satin! You're good enough to eat!'

One day, during a rare evening off work, Lala dressed in her Sunday best and a parasol and promenaded down the main avenue, past the white Viceroy's Palace (where, she'd heard, Ariadna had shocked the officers' wives with her bare shoulders and her frenzied dancing). The Tiflis streets smelt of lilac and lily of the valley. She passed theatres, opera houses and mansions on her way to Yerevan Square.

She'd been warned to be careful of the square and she soon realized why. The noisy, filthy side streets seethed with Turks, Persians, Georgians and mountain tribesmen in the brightest and wildest costumes, wielding daggers and blunderbusses. Urchins or *kintos* scampered through the crowds. Watersellers and porters pushed barrows. Officers walked their ladies but there were no women on their own. Barely had Lala stepped into the square when she was surrounded by a mob of urchins and salesmen, shouting in their own languages, all offering their wares – carpets, watermelons, pumpkin seeds and lobio beans. A fight broke out between a Persian waterseller and a Georgian urchin; a Chechen drew a dagger. It was early evening and still boiling hot. Jostled and harassed, with sweat pouring down her face, Lala was afraid. Then, just as she began to panic, the crowd parted and she found herself being pulled into a phaeton carriage.

'Mrs Lewis,' said Samuil Zeitlin, in an English blazer and white trousers, 'you're brave but silly venturing out here on your own. Would you like to see the Armenian Bazaar? It's not safe for a lady on her own but it's most exotic: would you join me?' She noticed he carried a cane with a wolf's head.

'Thank you, but I should be getting back to Sashenka.'

'It's a joy to me, Mrs Lewis, that you so treasure my only child but she'll be fine with Shifra for an hour,' said her master. 'Are you all right? Then let's stroll. You'll be safe with me.'

Zeitlin helped her down from the phaeton and they plunged into the wild crowd. Urchins offered Georgian snacks, Persians in fezes poured water from wineskins; Russian officers in jodhpurs and gold-buttoned tunics strode past; Circassian tribesmen with sabres and coats with pouches for bullets dismounted from their tough ponies. The sounds of hawkers shouting, 'Cool water, over here!' and the smells of fresh bread, cooking vegetables and heaps of spices were intoxicating.

Zeitlin showed her the steep alleyways and dark corners of the bazaar where bakers baked flat Georgian *lavashi*, Armenians displayed *kindjal* daggers and silver-chased saddles, Tatars sold sherbet prepared by their veiled women in back rooms, stopping sometimes to kneel on Persian carpets to pray to Allah, and a Mountain Jew played a hurdy-gurdy. As they walked, she put her hand through Zeitlin's arm: it seemed only natural. In a little café behind a stall selling spices, he bought her an iced sherbet and a glass of Georgian white wine that was stone cold, fruity, slightly sparkling.

It was dusk. The warm streets, steaming with the smells of hot Georgian cheesecake – *khachapuri* – and Armenian shashlik lamb, and reverberating with the laughter of women from balconies and the clip of horses on the cobbles, were still crowded and mysterious. Men brushed against her in the shadows. The wine made her head spin a little.

She dabbed her forehead with her handkerchief. 'Perhaps we should go home now.'

'But I haven't shown you old Tiflis yet,' he said, leading her down the hill, through tiny winding streets of crumbling houses with leaning balconies embraced by ancient vines. No one else was out in these streets and it was as if Zeitlin and she had stepped out of real life.

He opened an old gate, using a chunky key. A watchman with a spade-shaped white beard appeared and gave him a lantern. They were in a lost garden, draped in rich vines and honeysuckle that breathed out a heady perfume.

'I'm going to buy this house,' said Zeitlin. 'Doesn't it remind you of a Gothic novel?'

'Yes, yes,' she said, laughing. 'It makes me think of ghostly women in white gowns . . . What was that book by Wilkie collins?'

'Come and see the library. Do you like books, Audrey?'

'Oh yes, Monsieur Zeitlin . . .'

'Call me Samuil.'

They entered a cobbled courtyard, thick with creepers that reached up to the balconies. Zeitlin opened some bolted wooden doors into a cold stone hall decorated with bronze engravings. Inside, they found themselves in a high-ceilinged room panelled in dark wood and hung with dark lace curtains. He paced around lighting bronze lanterns with green shades until she could see this was a library. The Karelian pine bookshelves were full and more books were piled so high that in the midst of the room they formed a table and one could sit on them like chairs. The walls were covered with the strangest curiosities – the heads of wolves and bears, ancient maps of the world, portraits of kings and generals, Chechen sabres, medieval blunderbusses, pornographic postcards, socialist pamphlets, Orthodox icons, the cheap mixed with the priceless. A lost world. But it was the books in so many languages – Russian, English, French – that delighted her most.

'Take any books you want,' Zeitlin told her. 'While we're here, you must read whatever you like.' She followed him outside.

Their eyes met and glanced away and then met again in the darkening light of this perfume-heavy garden, the air so thick with the breath of vines and that special Georgian apple-and-almond scent of *tkemali* blossom that she could hardly breathe. She could smell his lemon cologne, his acrid cigar, and the sweet wine on his breath.

She would have done anything at that moment in the garden of the old house in Tiflis, anything he asked of her – yet just when she thought he was going to kiss her, he'd stepped back abruptly and left the garden. They hailed a phaeton on Golovinsky Prospect.

Next morning, when she brought Sashenka in to see Zeitlin at breakfast – Madame of course was still sleeping – Lala was grateful that he had not touched her. Giving her a distant smile and a 'Morning, Mrs Lewis', he kissed his daughter and returned to reading the shipping prices in his *Black Sea Gazette*. Neither of them had ever mentioned that evening again.

Since then, Lala's days had been full of Sashenka and she had no time or inclination for gentlemen friends. But recently, Sashenka had grown up much too fast. The Silberkind had darkened and slimmed down, becoming quiet and thoughtful. 'You and me will never marry, will we, Lala?' she had once said.

'Of course not.'

'Promise?'

'Promise.'

Lala did not understand politics but lately she realized that Karl Marx had taken her place in Sashenka's heart and she knew this was a bad, dangerous thing and it filled her with sorrow. She blamed that cripple with the trumpeting voice, Mendel.

Often, when she had turned out the oil lamp in her little room at the top of the house on Greater Maritime Street, her sleep was interrupted by dreams, wonderful dreams, of that moment with the master in that Georgian garden. As she turned over in bed, her skin flushed, and she imagined her breath against his chest, his lips touching her breasts, his hand between her thighs. Sometimes she awoke trembling all over.

And then, out of the blue, Zeitlin had invited her to the Donan.

'I really want my daughter back and you know her better than anyone,' he had said. 'Let's meet outside the house and plan her future. It's too late to enrol her in the Gymnasium on Gagarin Street. I was thinking of Professor Raev's Academy on Gorokhovaya . . .'

How differently things had turned out. At the restaurant he had never mentioned Sashenka. It had been like one of her disturbing dreams – yet Lala knew it was wrong and it alarmed her. She needed stability. If the master became reckless, what would happen to the household, to her, to Sashenka?

Lala feared change. The start of the war had been thrilling: she had stood among hundreds of thousands of peasants, workers, maids and countesses on Palace Square. She had seen the Tsar, Tsarina, the pretty Grand Duchesses and the little Heir on the balcony of the Winter Palace, blessing the crowd. Lala, now almost a Russian, had sung the Russian anthem and rejoiced as the recruits marched down Nevsky singing *'Nightingale, nightingale, you little bird!'*

Now she sensed something terrible was about to happen to her adopted country, yet it was too late for her to return home; she was too worldly, with her fluent Russian and visits to Biarritz and Baku; too set in her ways to start again in another household, and too attached to Sashenka to mother another child. She had saved a lot but not enough to live on.

She saw the bread queues in the streets, and the fast women outside the casinos and nightclubs of St Petersburg. She read in the newspapers how the armies were retreating, how the Germans had conquered Poland and many of Zeitlin's forests. She had to be civil to Ariadna's parents, who were camping in the house, talking in guttural Yiddish and chanting in Hebrew. The Tsar was at the front. Her hero Lord Kitchener, victor over the Mahdi and the Boers, had set out to visit Russia but his ship had hit a mine and he had drowned. But she still believed that, even though there might be trouble, her Samuil, her baron, would get them all through it.

In all these years, Lala had kept herself to herself, knowing her responsibilities, living modestly, already a spinster destined for a solitary old age, the ghost in the attic of a grand family. Like Shifra, in fact. And yet, well concealed beneath her dutiful blandness, like a frothy brook rushing down a mountainside under a carapace of thick ice, her blood was foaming. That night, as she prepared for bed, she replayed her teatime encounter with the baron. Curiously unembarrassed, they had lain together naked in the *kabinet* at the Donan.

'I'm divorcing Ariadna,' he said afterwards. 'Marry me, will you?'

For so long her body had been untouched, ignored, that every slightest caress, inside and out, had left marks as if tiny bee-stings had grazed her skin.

Now, as she looked at herself in the little mirror in her well-ordered bedroom, she could feel, deliciously, where he had been. Her skin scintillated. Unused, unknown muscles in tender places fluttered like captive butterflies. Her legs kept turning to rubber. As she waited for Sashenka to return, she tried to read a new book from England but she had to put it down.

She trembled inside and out with the wildest joy.

The bell suddenly rang in her room. This was unusual. As Lala came out, she heard a woman shouting and ran downstairs. Sashenka, pale and drained, stood in the lobby with the front door open, and a bedraggled, murmuring Ariadna reclined on a chair with her head in her hands.

'Oh Lala, thank God you're here. Help us to the bedroom. Then – let me think – call the maids and Dr Gemp.' Sashenka paused, then looked at Lala. 'Where's my father?'

CHAPTER 25

Captain Sagan stood wearily at the window of the safehouse on Gogol Street, lighting a thin cigar. It was a new year but the Russian defeats were worsening. He took a pinch of cocaine from his snuffbox and rubbed it into his gums. Instantly the blood fountained through his veins and his fatigue was transformed into a roaring optimism that galloped through his temples.

In the early hours of a January night, lanterns blinked across the Neva from the ramparts of the Peter and Paul Fortress. To his right, along the Embankment, the lights burned in the Winter Palace too, although the Tsars had not lived there since 1905. The Empress lived outside the city at Tsarskoe Selo and the Emperor at headquarters near the Front. But the fortress represented the power of the autocracy: in its church lay buried Peter the Great, Catherine and their successors all the way down to the present Emperor's father. But it was a prison too: the freezing cells of the Trubetskoy Bastion held the anarchists, nihilists and socialists he himself had trapped.

He heard the door click. Footsteps behind him.

Perhaps it was her? Or was it one of their assassins? One day, that click and this view might be the last thing his senses recorded before the shot that blew off the back of his head. It might even be her foolish finger on the trigger. But this was the Superlative Game, the risk of the life he led, the crusading work he did, his service to the Motherland. He believed in God, believed that he would go to Heaven: remove God and his son Jesus Christ and there was nothing, just chaos and sin. If he died now, he would never see his wife again. Yet it was meetings like this in the fathomless night that made his life worth living.

He did not turn round. Thrilling to the sight of the red Menshikov Palace, the fortress, the frozen river, Peter's city, he waited. He knew it was her coming into the room behind him, sitting on the divan. He could almost taste her.

Plainly dressed in a grey skirt and white blouse, like a virginal teacher, Sashenka was looking at a book. Sagan marvelled at how she had changed since her arrest. Although her hair was pulled back into a severe bun and her drawn face bereft of any make-up, this only made those dove-grey eyes more intense, those little islands of freckles all the more exquisite. The less flirtatious she was, the more she concealed her figure, the more he looked at her when she was looking away. She seemed to him even more compelling . . . yes, even beautiful.

'So, Comrade Petro' – that was what she now

called him – 'have you got something for us or not? Is the samovar boiling? Can I have some tea?'

Sagan made the *chai*. They had met often, and become quite informal. He could not know whether she was meeting him because she was beginning to like him or because the Party had ordered her to do so. We men are absurd, he thought, even as he hoped it was the former. It was fine to be attracted to her, even if she was barely a woman. But he did not need to remind himself that to become attached in any way, even fond, let alone in love, could risk not just his career but his sacred mission in life. He knew the rules. If Mendel was pulling the strings, the Bolshevik cripple would want Sagan to lust after her. This must never happen. It never would. Sagan was always in control.

'Happy New Year, Zemfira,' he said and he kissed her cheeks three times. 'How was the coming of 1917 in your house?'

'Joyful. Our house was more like a sanatorium this year.'

'How's your mother?'

'Ask your spies if you really want to know.' Accustomed to conspiracy, she seemed more confident than ever. Yet he was sure that, since Rasputin's death, she had started to trust him, in spite of her Bolshevik vigilance. When they met the night after Rasputin's death, she had thanked him. For a moment he even thought she might hug him in her prim comradely way, but she did not. Yet they kept meeting.

'Is the baroness's opium working? Is she trying hypnosis? I understand it works.'

'I don't care,' she replied. 'She's better, I think. She's getting another dress made and grumbling about Uncle Gideon's outrages.'

'And the divorce?'

'Papa should divorce her but I don't think he'll dare. She's a lost soul. She believes in nothing but pleasure. I'm hardly at home now.' There was a pause. 'The Party's growing. Have you noticed? Have you seen the bread queues? There are fights every day for the last loaves.'

He sighed, suddenly craving more cocaine, fighting an urge to tell her more about himself, more of what he knew. He was surprised by a wave of hopelessness that seemed to blow in from the streets of the city and sweep over him. Were Tsar, Empire and Orthodoxy already lost?

'You know the truth from your reports,' she said, leaning forward, 'and I know you sympathize with us. Come on, Petro. Show me a little of yourself – or I might get bored and never meet you again. Tell me something I don't know. Tell me what your reports say?'

The perceptive grey eyes studied him unforgivingly, he thought.

He said nothing.

She raised her eyebrows and gestured with her hands. Then, jumping up, she gathered her karakul coat and *shapka* and headed for the door. She opened it.

'Wait,' he said, his head tightening like a vice. He did not want her to go. 'I've got a headache. Let me have a toke of my tonic.'

'Go right ahead.' She watched him open his crested silver box, an heirloom set with diamonds, and, wetting his finger, take a thick layer of white powder and rub it into his gums. His arteries distended, the blood gushed once more to his temples, and he wondered if she could see the seething swell of his lips.

'Our reports,' he started to tell her, 'warn the Tsar of revolution. I've just written one that reads: *If food supplies are not improved, it will be hard to enforce law and order on the streets of Petrograd. The garrison remains loyal but . . .* Why do we bother? The new government's a joke. Sturmer, Trepov, now this antique Prince Golitsyn, are pygmies and crooks. Rasputin's murder hasn't solved anything. We need a new start. I don't agree with every-thing you believe in, but some of it makes sense . . .'

'Interesting.' She stood right in front of him so that he thought he could smell her – was it Pears lavender soap? Her finger stroked her lips. He understood that she had grown up faster than he had realized. 'We've been back and forth, haven't we, Comrade Petro? But now we're getting impa-tient! If you think I like meeting you, you might just be right. We might almost be friends . . . but are we? Some of my comrades don't think I should see you any more. If you really sympathize with us, there are things we need to know. "It's a waste of time," my comrades say. "Sagan wouldn't give us ice in winter." In any case, you know your work's all for nothing. Your world's about to end. You need to give us something to persuade us to spare you.'

'You're too optimistic, Sashenka, deluded. I don't think much of the standard of your newspapers but, between ourselves, they tell the truth about the situation in the factories and at the front. I've agonized about this. But I might have something for you.'

'You do?' Sashenka's smile as she said this made it worthwhile. She tossed off her coat and sat again, still in her *shapka*.

Not for the first time, Sagan wrestled with the infinite possibilities of who was playing whom. Sashenka's new confidence informed him that she was still telling Mendel about their meetings. Sagan was disappointed that she was not coming just out of affection – maybe he was losing his touch – but she was surely a little fond of him? 'Almost friends,' she had said. In spite of himself, the secret policeman felt a tinge of hurt. But they talked about their families, poetry, even health.

So how much did she tell Mendel? He hoped she was keeping back their closeness, because this was how it worked: the holding back of small things led to small lies and then the holding back of larger things led to big lies – this was how he recruited his double agents. He wanted to destroy

Mendel and Sashenka was the tool to do it. Duplicity, not honesty, was his métier – but if he was honest for once, she was not only a tool. She was his delight.

'Listen carefully,' he said. 'They're planning a raid tomorrow night on your printing press down the road. You need to move it. I don't need to know where.'

She tried to conceal her excitement from him, but the way she knitted her eyebrows to assume a military briskness made him want to laugh.

'Are you leading this raid?' she asked.

'No, it's a Gendarmerie operation. To find out the details, I had to promise to trade some information in return.'

'That's presumptuous, Comrade Petro.'

He flicked his wrist impatiently. 'All intelligence work is a marketplace, Sashenka. This has kept me up night after night. I can't sleep. I live on Dr Gemp's powder. I want to help your Party, the people, Russia, but everything inside me rebels against giving you anything. You know I'm risking all by telling you this?'

Sashenka turned to leave. 'If it's a lie, this is over and they'll want your head. If your spooks follow me from here, we'll never meet again. Do we understand each other?'

'And if it's true?' he called after her.

'Then we'll meet again very soon.'

CHAPTER 26

Agentle sepia light shone through the clouds, reflected off the snow, and burst brighter through the curtains: the opium sailed through Ariadna's veins. Dr Gemp had called to give her the injection. Her head dropped on to the pillow and she drifted in and out of dreams: Rasputin and she were together in Heaven, he was kissing her forehead; the Empress was inspecting them, dressed in her grey nursing outfit. Rasputin held her hand and, for the first time in her life, she was truly happy and secure.

In her bedroom, she could hear soft voices speaking in Yiddish. Her parents were sitting with her. 'Poor child,' murmured her mother. 'Is she possessed by a dybbuk?'

'Everything is God's will, even this,' replied her father. 'That's the point of free will. We can only ask for his mercy . . .' Ariadna could hear the creak of the leather strap as the rabbi tied his phylactery on to his arm and he switched to Hebrew. He was reciting the Eighteen Benedictions and this familiar, reassuring chant bore her like a magic carpet back in time . . .

A young and handsome Samuil Zeitlin was standing in the muddy lane outside the Talmudic Studyhouse, near the workshop of Lazar the cobbler in the little Jewish-Polish town of Turbin, not far from Lublin. He was asking for her hand in marriage. She shrugged at first: he was not a Prince Dolgoruky or even a Baron Rothschild, not good enough for her – but then who would be? Her father shouted, 'The Zeitlin boy's a heathen! He doesn't eat or dress like one of us: does he keep kosher? Does he know the Eighteen Benedictions? That father of his with his bow ties and holidays in Bad Ems: they're apostates!'

Then she was circling the Jewish wedding canopy – the chuppah – seven times; Samuil was smashing a wine glass with a decisive stamp of his boot. Her new husband was borne aloft by the singing Hasids, with an expression on his face that said: I just pray I never have to see these primitive fanatics ever again – but I've got her! I've got her! Tonight I make love to the most beautiful girl in the Pale! Tomorrow, Warsaw! The day after, Odessa. And she would escape Turbin, at last, for ever.

Then it was years later and she was caressing Captain Dvinsky in a suite at the Bristol in Paris, where she amazed even that connoisseur of flesh with her depravities. In a torn camisole, she was on all fours, pressing her loins down on to his face, smearing his face, revolving like a stripper, delighted by the wantonness of it, hissing swear-words in

Polish, obscenities in Yiddish. Even now, waves of lust, the stroking of naked men, the kisses of women, washed over her.

She sat up in bed, cold, sober. She thought she saw the Elder: yes, there was his beard and his glittering eyes at the end of the bed. 'Is it you, Grigory?' she asked aloud. But then she realized that it was a combination of the curtain pelmet and a dress on a stand that somehow suggested a tall, thin man with a beard. She was alone and clear-headed suddenly.

Rasputin, who offered me a new road to happiness, is dead, she thought. Samuil, whose love and wealth were the pillars of my rickety palace, is divorcing me. Sashenka hates me – and who can blame her? My Hasidic parents shame me and I am ashamed of my shame. My whole life, every step of the way, has been a fiasco. My happiness has been tottering on a tightrope, only to tumble through the air. Even my pleasures are like the moment that high-wire artiste starts to tremble and loses her footing . . .

I mocked my father's world of holiness and superstition. Perhaps my mother was right: was I cursed since birth? I mocked Fate because I had everything. Does the Evil Eye possess me?

Ariadna lay back on the pillow, alone and adrift on the oceans like a ship without a crew.

CHAPTER 27

Sashenka left an emergency message for Mendel at Lordkipadze, the Georgian pharmacy on Alexandrovsky Prospect, and then walked home down Nevsky. The clouds billowed into creamy cauliflowers that hung low over the city. The ice that curled from the drainpipes and the roofs was stiffening. The thermometer was sinking to minus twenty. In the workers' districts, the sirens and whistles blared. Strikes had started to spread from factory to factory.

On Nevsky, right in the centre, clerks, workers, even bourgeois housewives queued outside the bakeries for bread. Two women rolled around in the sludge fighting for the last loaves: a working woman repeatedly hit the other in the face, and Sashenka heard the crack as her nose broke.

At Yeliseyev's Grocery Store, where the Zeitlins ordered their food, Sashenka watched as workers burst in and grabbed cakes and fruit. The shop assistant was bludgeoned.

That night, she could not even pretend to sleep. Her head was buzzing. The anger of the streets replayed in her mind. Outside, the sirens of the

Vyborg echoed across the Neva, like the calling of whales.

She rose from her bed, and in the early hours Comrade Molotov met her at the coachmen's café outside the Finland Station.

'Comrade Mendel is busy now. He sent me.' Molotov was humourless and stern but also meticulous and he listened carefully to Sashenka's tip-off.

'Your s-s-source is r-reliable?' Molotov stammered, his forehead bulging.

'I think so.'

'Thank you, c-c-comrade. I'll get to work.'

At dawn, Comrades Vanya and Satinov were already dismantling the printing press. Sashenka and other comrades removed the parts in beer barrels, milk churns, coal sacks. The bulky press itself was placed in a coffin, collected by a stolen undertaker's hearse and accompanied by a carriage of weeping (Bolshevik) relatives in black to the new site in Vyborg.

At dusk the following afternoon, Mendel and Sashenka climbed the stairs of an office building down the street from the printing press. For Mendel, every step was an effort as he dragged his fortified boot behind him.

They came out on the roof and Sashenka gave Mendel one of her Crocodile cigarettes, its gold tip incongruous beside his worker's cap and rough leather coat. Together, they watched as three carriages of grey-clad police and two carloads of gendarmes pulled up outside the cellar and broke down the door.

'Good work, Comrade Snowfox,' said Mendel. 'You were right.'

She flushed with pride. She really was an asset to the Party, not the spoilt child of the degenerate classes.

'Do I continue to meet Sagan?'

Mendel's eyes, magnified by his bottle-glass lenses, pivoted towards her. 'I suppose he's in love with you.'

She laughed and shook her head simultaneously. 'With me? You must be joking. No one looks at *me* like that. Sagan talks mostly about poetry. He really knows his stuff. He was helpful about Mama but he's very proper. And I'm a Bolshevik, comrade, I don't flirt.'

'Fucking poetry! Don't be naïve, girl. So he *lusts* after you!'

'No! Certainly not!' She blushed with confusion. 'But he sympathizes with us. That's why he tipped us off.'

'They always say that. Sometimes it's even true. But don't trust any of his *shtik*.' Mendel often used the Yiddish of his childhood. While Ariadna had completely lost the accent, Sashenka noticed that Mendel still spoke Russian with a strong Polish-Jewish intonation.

'If you're right about his immorality, comrade, I don't think I should meet Sagan again. He sent me a note this morning, inviting me to take a sleigh ride with him in the countryside. I said no of course and now I certainly shan't meet him.'

'Don't be such a *schlamazel*, Sashenka,' he replied. 'You don't know what's best here, girl. Beware bourgeois morality. We'll decide what's immoral and what isn't. If the Party asks you to cover yourself in shit, you do it! If he desires you, so much the better.'

Sashenka felt even more flustered. 'You mean . . .'

'Go on the sleigh ride,' he boomed, exasperated. 'Meet the scum as often as it takes.'

'But he needs something to show for it too.'

'We'll give him a morsel or two. But in return, we want a gold nugget. Get me the name of the traitor who betrayed the press in the first place. Without that name, this operation is a failure. The Party will be disappointed. Be vigilant. *Tak!* That's it.' Mendel's face was livid with the cold. 'Let's go down before we freeze. How's your mother coping with the divorce?'

'I never see her. Dr Gemp says she's hysterical *and* melancholic. She's on chloral, bromine, opium. Father wants her to try hypnotism.'

'Is he going to marry Mrs Lewis?'

'What?' Sashenka felt this like a punch in the belly. Her father and Lala? What was he talking about? But Mendel was already on his way downstairs.

194

The factory whistles started up again across the city, yet the black slate of the rooftops revealed none of the seething furies beneath. The world really was going mad, she thought.

CHAPTER 28

The next day was warmer. The sun and the moon watched each other suspiciously across a milky sky. The sparse clouds resembled two sheep and a ram, horns and all, on a snowy field. The factories were on strike.

As she took the tram to the Finland Station, Sashenka saw crowds crossing the bridges from the factories, demonstrating for bread for the third day running. The demonstration had started on Thursday, International Women's Day, and grown since then.

'Arise, you starvelings, from your slumbers!' the crowds chanted, waving their red banners. 'Down with autocracy! Give us bread and peace!'

The Cossacks tried to turn them back at the Alexander Bridge but tens of thousands marched anyway. Sashenka saw women in peasant shawls smash the windows of the English Shop and help themselves to food: 'Our men are dying at the front! Give us bread! Our children are starving!' There were urchins on the streets now, creatures with the bodies of children but with swollen bellies and the faces of old monkeys. One sat on the street corner singing and playing his concertina:

Here I am abandoned, an orphan, with no one to look after me,
And I will die before long and there'll be no one to pray at my grave,
Only the nightingale will sing sometimes on the nearest tree.

Sashenka gave the boy some money and a Red pamphlet: 'After the Revolution,' she told him, 'you'll have bread; you'll be the masters; read Marx and you'll understand. Start with *Das Kapital* and then—' But the boy had scampered off.

Sashenka had no special orders from the Party. At first light, she'd checked with Shlyapnikov at the Shirokaya safehouse. 'The demonstrations are a waste of time, comrade,' he insisted. 'Don't squander any of our leaflets. This'll lead to nought like all the other riots.' On Friday, a police officer had been killed by the workers on the bridge – and a mob had broken into Filippov's, the patisserie where Delphine the cook bought Baron Zeitlin's millefeuille.

Now the authorities were striking back. The city was filled with Cossacks and soldiers, and it seemed to Sashenka like an armed camp. Every side street, every bridge was guarded by machine-gun nests and armoured cars; squadrons of horsemen massed on the squares; horse manure steamed on the snow.

The theatres were still playing and Ariadna was so improved that she and Zeitlin were off to the Alexandrinsky to see Lermontov's *Masquerade*, a most avant-garde production. The Donan and the Contant were still crowded, and the orchestras played waltzes and tangos at the Europa and Astoria hotels.

Sashenka was meeting Sagan. She hurried first to the safehouse at 153 Nevsky but Mendel, who was with Shlyapnikov and Molotov, ordered her to calm down. 'Give these workers a few shots over their heads and a loaf of bread and the movement will be gone.' The others agreed. Perhaps they were right, Sashenka thought uncertainly.

At the Finland Station, Sashenka checked her police tails out of habit. There was one spook who fitted the bill but she lost him easily before she caught the train, travelling third class. In the cold, the steam seemed to wheeze out of the train, whirling around it like a wizard's spell.

She had arranged to meet Sagan at Beloostrov, the small town nearest the Finnish border. When she arrived – the only passenger to leave the carriage – Sagan was waiting in a troika, a sleigh with three horses, smoking a cigar, shrouded in furs. She climbed in and he covered their laps with the fur blanket. The coachman spat out a spinning green gobbet of phlegm, cracked his whip and they were off. Sashenka remembered such trips with Lala in the family sleigh with its ivory fittings, the family crest on the doors, the sable rug. Now this flimsy sleigh, creaking and clattering, flew over the fields, the coachman in his sheepskin and fur hood leaning to one side, drunkenly flicking his whip over the mangy rumps of the skinny piebalds. Every now and then he talked to the horses or his passengers but it was hard to hear him over the swish of the sleigh and the thud of the hooves.

'Giddy-up . . . Oats . . . prices rising . . . Oats . . .'

'Shouldn't you be in Piter fighting the wicked pharaohs?' Sagan asked her.

'The workers are just hungry, not rebels at all. Aren't you worried though?'

He shook his head. 'There'll be riots but nothing more.'

'The Party agrees with you.' She peered up into Sagan's face. He looked exhausted and anxious – the strain of his double life and miserable marriage, the headaches and insomnia, the rising turbulence in the city, all seemed to be catching up with him. She shook her head at Mendel's accusations. How could he know what Sagan felt when he had never met him and certainly never seen them together? No, Sagan had become a sort of friend – he alone understood the pain of having a mother like Ariadna. She felt that he liked her too, for her own sake, but *not* like *that*! Not at all! Sagan was not even suited to police work. He was much more like a vague poet than a frightening policeman with his feathery blond hair that he wore much too long – and yet it suited him. They were enemies in many ways, she knew that, but their understanding was based on mutual respect and shared ideas and tastes. She had a serious mission and when it was over they might never see each other again. But she was glad Mendel had ordered her to see Sagan again. Very glad. She had family news to tell him and who else could she confide in?

'Something has happened at home,' she began. There was no harm in recounting harmless gossip. 'Mrs Lewis! My Lala! Mendel has a spy in the Donan. That's how I discovered. When I confronted Papa, he blushed and denied it and looked away and then finally admitted that he had considered marrying her for *me*, to make me a happier home. As if that would make the slightest difference to my life! But now he says he's not going to divorce Mama. She's too fragile. I asked Lala and she hugged me and told me she refused him on the spot. They're all such children, Comrade Petro. Their world's about to end, the inevitable dialectic's about to crush them and they're still playing like that orchestra on the *Titanic*.'

'Are you hurt?' he asked, leaning towards her. She noticed his blond moustache was cut just like her father's.

'Of course not,' she answered huskily, 'but I never thought of Lala like that!'

'Governesses are prone to it. I had my first love affair with my sister's governess,' said Sagan.

'Did you?' She was suddenly disappointed in him. 'And how's your wife?'

He shook his head. 'I'm spiritually absent from my home. I come and go like a ghost. I find myself doubting everything I once believed in.'

'Lala was my confidante. Who do you talk to?'

'No one. Not my wife. Sometimes I think, well, maybe *you're* the only person I can be myself with because we're half-strangers, half-friends, don't you see?'

Sashenka smiled. 'What a pair we are!' She closed her eyes and let the wind with its refreshing droplets of snow sprinkle her face.

'There!' shouted Sagan. He pointed at an inn just ahead.

'Right, master,' cried the sleigh-driver and whipped the horses.

'We're almost there,' Sagan said, touching her arm.

A tiny wooden cottage, with colourful wooden carvings hanging from its roof, stood all alone in the middle of the snowfields with only a few birches on either side like bodyguards. Sashenka thought the place belonged in a Snow Queen fairy tale.

The sleigh swished to a stop, the horses' nostrils flared and steaming in the cold. The wooden door opened, and a fat peasant with a jet-black beard came out in a bearskin kaftan and soft boots to hand her down from the sleigh.

Inside, the 'inn' was more like a peasant *izba*. The 'restaurant' was a single room with a traditional Russian stove, on top of which a very old man with a shaggy white beard lay full-length, snoring noisily in his socks. Inside the half-open stove, Sashenka saw game sizzling on a spit. The black-bearded peasant showed them to a rough wooden table and thrust a generous shot of *cha-cha* into their hands.

'To a strange pair!' said Sagan and they drank. She had never been out for a meal with a man before. The *cha-cha* burned in Sashenka's belly like a red-hot bullet, and this unlikely idyll – the open fire, the sleeping old man and the aromatic game in the stove – softened her concentration. She imagined that they were the only people alive in the whole of the frozen north. Then she mentally shook herself, to keep her wits about her. Joking with Sagan, whom he seemed to know, the peasant served them roast goose in a piping-hot casserole, so well done that the fat and flesh almost dripped off the bones to flavour a mouth-watering beetroot, garlic and potato broth. They so enjoyed the food that they almost forgot the Revolution, and just made small talk. There was no dessert, and the old man never awoke. Eventually they left, very satisfied, after another *cha-cha*.

'Your tip checked out, Petro,' said Sashenka as the sleigh sped over the featureless snowfields.

'It was hard to give you that.'

'But it wasn't enough. We want the name of the man who betrayed us.'

'I might get it for you. But if we're going to keep meeting, I need to show my superiors something . . .'

She let the silence develop as she prepared herself, excited by the danger of their game. 'All right,' she said. 'There is something. Gurstein escaped from exile.'

'We know that.'

'He's in Piter.'

'That we guessed.'

'Well, do you want to find him?'

He nodded.

'Try the Kiev boarding house, Room 12.' This was the response she'd rehearsed with Mendel, who had warned her that she would have to trade some information of her own. Gurstein was apparently expendable.

Sagan did not seem impressed. 'He's a Menshevik, Sashenka. I want a Bolshevik.'

'Gurstein escaped with Senka Shashian from Baku.'

'The insane brigand who robbed banks for Stalin?'

'He's in Room 13. *You* owe me, Comrade Petro. If this was known, the Party'd kill me by morning. Now give me the name of the traitor who betrayed the printing press.'

There was just the crispness of blades slicing frozen snow, and Sashenka could almost feel

Sagan weighing up the price of a man's life versus the value of an agent.

'Verezin,' he said at last.

'The concierge of the Horse Guards barracks?'

'Surprised?'

'Nothing surprises me,' Sashenka said, exultantly.

The sky was furrowed with scarlet, as if ploughed with blood. Rabbits jumped out ahead of the horses and crisscrossed each other, making jubilant leaps. What joy! Sagan gave orders to the coachman, who whipped the horses.

Sashenka sat back and closed her eyes. She had the name. Her mission was successful. The Party would be pleased. She had got what Mendel wanted – not bad, she decided, for a Smolny girl! Somehow, together, she and Sagan had delivered. They had shared the adrenalin that all operatives feel after a successful mission. She had tricked him and, for whatever reason, he had given her his nugget of gold.

A cottage appeared in the distance, probably on the edge of some estate. The temperature was falling, and the ice was stiffening again. A clump of pines looked as if they were made of tarnished silver.

'See, there!' said Sagan, taking her gloved hand in his own. 'Isn't it beautiful? Far away from the struggle in the city. I wanted to show you an exquisite little place that I love.'

'There you are, *barin*,' said the coachman, raising his eyebrows and spitting. 'Just as you ordered.'

'I could live here for ever,' said Sagan passionately,

pulling off his *shapka*, his flaxen locks flopping over his eyes. 'I might escape out here. I could be happy here, don't you think?'

A little curl of smoke puffed out of the distant tin chimney. Sagan took her hand and slipped her glove off. Their hands, dry and warm, cleaved together, breathing each other's skin. Then he took her left hand and slipped it inside his own glove, where her fingers rested closely against his, buried in kid leather and the softest rabbit fur. It seemed impertinent, yes, and horribly intimate, but she found it delicious too. She gasped. The tender skin of her palm seemed to become unbearably sensitive, glowing and prickling against his rough skin. She felt a flush rising up her neck, and withdrew her hand from his glove abruptly.

She could feel his eyes on her, but she looked away. That, she decided, had been a step too far.

'Faster! *Bistro!*' Sagan barked at the driver. The three horses jumped forward and suddenly the driver lost control. The sleigh bounced left and right, the driver shouting, but the snow was uneven, tipping them one way, then the other and finally flipping the sleigh in a powdery tornado of whirling snow until Sashenka found herself flying through the air.

She landed in a soft drift, face down, and was still for a moment. Sagan was close to her but not moving. Was he alive? What if he was dead? She sat up. The horses were still galloping away, the driver chasing after them and the sleigh upside down. Sagan was still, his face covered in snow.

'Petro!' she called out, crawling over to him. She touched the dimple in his chin.

Sagan sat up laughing, wiping the snow off his long narrow face.

'You gave me a shock,' she said.

'I thought we were *both* dead,' he replied, and she laughed too.

'Look at us!' she said, 'we're soaked . . .'

'. . . and cold,' he said, looking for the sleigh. 'And I fear quite alone!'

She saw that his dark pupils were dilated with the excitement of the crash. She put his hat back on his head and they could not stop laughing, like children. Sitting there in the midst of the snow-fields, the cottage still far away, the sleigh invisible, he moved his head to rest on her shoulder just as she did the same and they bumped heads, then looked at one another.

Without missing a beat, he kissed her on the lips. No one had ever kissed her before. Thinking of the Party, relishing her success, and remembering that perhaps Mendel was right after all, perhaps Sagan did like her, she allowed him to press his lips on hers. His tongue opened her mouth and licked her lips, teeth, tongue. Her lips tingled and she became drowsy and dreamy. For a moment, just a moment, she closed her eyes and let her head rest against his, and her hand did what it had always wanted to do: stroke the pale hair that reminded her of candyfloss. They had shared personal confidences – the poetry, his marriage and headaches, her family – but nothing so all-embracing as the Superlative Game of conspiracy. The deadly exchange of information formed the climax of a slow, voluptuous polka on the thinnest ice. Sashenka was dizzy and shaky, yet sparks of nervous excitement and a flick of sensuous heat flashed through her.

'Here we are, *barin*!' cried the sleigh-driver, whose entire beard was frosted like a fungus. He had righted his sledge and driven his troika of lathered horses in a big circle to pick them up again. 'Apologies for the bump but, well, no broken bones, I see. A picture of health!' and he cackled coarsely. Sagan's skin was warm, prickly, rough on her cheeks and chin. It burned her – and she broke away. 'Whoa!' cried the driver. The sleigh came to a halt beside them with a slushy crunching that sprinkled a shower of frozen stars on to their faces.

Sagan helped her up and brushed the snow off her and then handed her back on to the sleigh. Her hands and knees were quivering. She wiped her lips with her sleeve. She was unsure of herself, unsettled.

Moments later, they arrived at the cottage. Spears of ice with fine points hung down from the eaves, and intricate blossoms of frost made opulent patterns on the windows. The nailed wooden door opened and a smiling pink-cheeked peasant girl in a sheepskin kaftan came out, bearing a tray with two glasses of *gogol-mogol*. The glowering sky spread its soft blanket over the snow, turning it a deep purplish blue.

Afterwards, Sagan and Sashenka parted at the station.

She had a rash on her chin. She touched it with her fingertips and, remembering his lips against hers, she shivered.

CHAPTER 29

Captain Sagan watched Sashenka's little train pull away and gather speed, its steam billowing like the sultan-spike of a gendarme's helmet.

He showed his pass to the stationmaster, who was almost overcome with excitement as Sagan commandeered the fool's cosy office. Warming himself by the Dutch stove and helping himself to a shot of cognac, he wrote a report to his boss, General Globachev.

Sagan's temples were tightening, always the start of a reverberating headache. He quickly rubbed some of the medicinal powder on to his gums then sniffed two tokes. Things were not going well. He and the general were more worried about St Petersburg than he had let on to Sashenka. But both men agreed that a crackdown and a dismissal of the Duma were necessary: it was time, he considered, for the Cossack to wield his *nagaika* whip. The coca tonic replaced his anxiety with a feeling of all-conquering satisfaction that drummed in his temples.

Ever since his days in the Corps de Pages, Sagan had been in the top stream, winner of the highest prize during the two years of courses at the School for Detectives. He had learned the anthropometric tables of the Bertillon system for describing the features of those under surveillance, won the bullseye prize in Captain Glasfedt's practical course on firearms and mastered the 'Instructions on Organizational Conduct of Internal Agents', which he had applied punctiliously to Sashenka. He had memorized the urbane orders of Colonel Zubatov, the genius of the Okhrana, who had written: *You should look on your informer as a mistress with whom you are involved in an adulterous affair.* It was indeed impossible to turn female revolutionaries into double agents without exploiting chivalry in some form, even if that meant what he called 'anti-chivalry' – allowing silly teenagers to believe they were serious intellectuals who would never contemplate the slightest flirtation, yet alone sexual approaches. Sagan had followed Zubatov's recommendations with one of his female double agents in the SRs and another in the Bolsheviks. Neither was a beauty but, in bed, the drama of espionage more than compensated for the often dull athletics.

Sagan always prepared himself meticulously for his meetings with Sashenka, listening to the latest tango, learning reams of that doggerel by Mayakovsky which had turned her head. Her devotion to Bolshevism made it child's play: the humourless ones were always the easiest to crack, he told himself. Like so many of the revolutionaries, she was a *zhyd*, a kike, one of that race of turncoats who supported either godless Marxism or the German Kaiser. He smiled at his own liberal posturing, he who believed so passionately in Tsar, Orthodoxy and Motherland, the old order.

Now, using the stationmaster's pen and ink, he started to write his report to the General:

Your Excellency, I am most satisfied with the case of Agent 23X ('Snowfox') who has finally started to prove useful. As Your Excellency knows, I have now met clandestinely with this member of the RSWP (Russian Socialist Workers' Party: Bolshevik faction) eleven times, counting the first interrogation. The hours of work have paid off and will yield considerable gains later. Using our surveillance teams of external agents, Snowfox's movements have enabled us to arrest three nihilists of middling rank and to track the new printing press.

The price for the recruitment of this agent has been 1. philosophical – her conviction of my sympathy for her cause and her person (the rescuing of her mother from the Dark One's apartment was particularly successful in gaining trust); and 2. tactical – the handover of the name of the doorman (new Party member codenamed Horseguards) which has cost our service nothing since we earlier failed to recruit him as an internal agent, despite the offer of the usual financial inducements

(100 roubles/month) as per P. Stolypin's 'Instructions on Organizational Conduct of Internal Agents'.

At today's meeting, the agent surrendered the name of two revolutionists, a Menshevik factionist and a Bolshevik terrorist, who had long been sought by the Security Sections of Baku, Moscow and Petrograd. I will organize surveillance according to General Trusevich's 'Instructions for External Surveillance' and arrest forthwith. I request your permission to continue to handle Agent 'Snowfox' in the future as I believe that her usefulness for the service depends on my management. It is possible that her Bolshevik handlers have ordered her to hand over these names but I believe that the threat of exposure to her own comrades will now make her submission easy to accomplish.

Our primary mission remains the arrest of Mendel Barmakid, her uncle (codename Clubfoot; alias Comrade Baramian, Comrade Furnace, etc.) and the Bolshevik faction's Petrograd Committee, but I have absolute confidence that this organization is now hopelessly broken and incapable of any threat in the short to medium term . . .

Poor little Sashenka, he thought smugly – yet in his heart he knew she was the brightest star in his firmament.

He did not look forward to seeing his wife or General Globachev. If he had had his way, he would have met Sashenka at the safehouse every night.

Her diffidence, those teenage doubts, her awkward stance, the prim way she dressed in grey serge, dreary wool stockings and buttoned blouses with her thick hair in a virginal Bolshevik bun, the absence of any make-up or even scent – all this had wearied him initially. But in recent weeks she had began to grow on him and now he looked forward to the smell of her fresh skin and her sumptuous hair when she was near him, the way her columbine eyes bored into him so intensely, her fingers touching her short upper lip when she talked about her mother, the way her slim body was shaping into a woman's curves that she was determined to conceal and scorn. And nothing was so adorable as the way she suppressed her humour and joie de vivre, knitting her brows to play the dour revolutionary. He laughed at the tricks of the Almighty, for, however matronly she wanted to be, God had given her features – those lips that never closed, those scathing grey eyes, that lush bosom – that undermined her wishes at every turn and made her even more delicious.

And when he had tasted her lips, his hands had actually started to shake. Her reluctance to return his kiss made her obvious enjoyment of it even more poignant and delightful. Or did I imagine that? he asked himself. Any man of almost forty would lose judgement when faced with that skin, those lips, and the husky bumble-bee voice he had come to know so well. He raised his hands and thought he could divine the scent of her skin, her neck . . .

Yet she was his agent. The cause, Tsar and Motherland, always came first. It was a desperate struggle for survival between good and evil and she was on the wrong side. If he had to . . . Well, he hoped it would never come to that. The Okhrana was special. The battle to defend the Empire was a war that had to be fought with merciless conspiracy – as his colleague General Batiushin had told him: 'All honour to him who dishonours his name and ends the case with silence as his only reward.' He wet his finger and dipped it into Dr Gemp's powder and applied cocaine to nose and gums. He chuckled to himself.

The door opened. A livid snout and ginger whiskers appeared, followed by a uniformed paunch and the rest of the stationmaster.

'Did you say something, Your Excellency?' he said. 'Anything I can do? A note to my superiors would be a help. I'd be so grateful . . .'

'Why not?'

'We hope you're destroying our enemies, German agents and *zhyd* nihilists!' The station-master rubbed his hands.

'Absolutely! When's the next train to the Finland Station? I have a report to file.'

'Five minutes, Your Excellency. God Save the Tsar!'

CHAPTER 30

The Grand Duke's crested Benz was already parked among the carriages outside the Radziwill Palace on Fontanka when Pantameilion's Delaunay swung into the forecourt, the chains wrapped around the wheels just gripping the ice. Samuil and Ariadna Zeitlin waited their turn while the French Embassy Renault dropped Ambassador Paleologue and his wife.

The Izmailovsky Guards in green tunics, the gendarmes with their sultan-spikes and the Cossacks in leather trousers and high furs, flicking their thick whips, bivouacked around bonfires in the squares and guarded the street corners. The air steamed with horse sweat and manure and sweet woodsmoke; the cobbles clattered with the clipclop of a thousand hooves, the rumble of howitzer carriages, the metallic rattle of rifles, horse tackle and scabbards.

The melody of waltzes and laughter wafted down the marble stairs of the palace. The Zeitlins greeted the French ambassador and his wife at the top of the steps. The foursome were just agreeing how quiet the city was when a gunshot echoed over the rooftops. Dogs howled, sirens wailed and somewhere out towards the Vyborg Side the city herself seemed to growl.

'How are you, dear Baron? Are you better, Baroness?' The French ambassador bowed, speaking fluent Russian.

'Much better, thank you. Did you hear that?' asked Ariadna, her eyes iridescent as whirlpools. 'A firework!'

'That was gunfire, Baroness, I fear,' replied the ambassador, immaculate in black coat, top hat and white tie. 'There it is again. The metal factory workers are marching in their hundreds of thousands from Petrograd, Vyborg and Narva.'

'I'm freezing,' shivered Ariadna.

'Let's go in,' said the Frenchwoman, taking her hand.

The ambassador's wife and Ariadna, both in floor-length furs, one in ermine, the other in seal, walked inside, handing their coats to the staff. Ariadna, like an angel stepping out of a fountain, emerged glistening and pale in a mauve brocade gown embroidered in diamonds with a high bosom and low-cut back. She embraced the richest couple in Lithuanian Poland, Prince and Princess Radziwill.

'You're so good to come, Ariadna, and you, Madame Paleologue, on such a night. We wondered whether to cancel but dearest Grand Duke Basil absolutely banned it. He said it was

216

our duty, yes, our duty. We've spoken to General Kabalov and he's most reassuring . . .'

More gunshots. Zeitlin and the ambassador remained outside on the steps, peering into the night. Puttering limousines and whispering sleighs dropped off the guests. Diamonds and emeralds hung like dewdrops on the ears of the women who moved like animals in their sleek furs. Perfume vied with the biting cold for possession of the air. Zeitlin lit a cigar and offered one to the ambassador.

They were both silent. The ambassador, knowing how prices were rocketing and the secret police warning of imminent unrest, was amazed to find ministers and Grand Dukes at play on a night like this.

Zeitlin was lost in his private thoughts. He had lived through riots, demonstrations, pogroms, two wars and the 1905 revolution, emerging richer and stronger each time. Things at home were calm again; his uncharacteristic flash of madness and doubt was over.

Dr Gemp's injections of opium had restored Ariadna; the divorce was off; Sashenka was enrolled in Professor Raev's classes, and Lala seemed calm and acquiescent. The only worry was Gideon. What was that scallywag, that *momzer*, up to?

CHAPTER 31

Gideon Zeitlin was on his way home, driven by Leonid the butler in the big touring car, the Russo-Balt, with two hundred roubles in his pocket. Cossacks and guardsmen had erected checkpoints around the official Liteiny cordon that guarded the General Staff, War Ministry and Winter Palace. But as Gideon crossed Nevsky, some workers threw stones at the car.

'Filthy speculator!' they shouted. 'We'll teach you to fleece the people.'

The stones drummed on the roof but Gideon, always slightly screwed even when sober, was not scared. 'Me? Of all people? It's my brother you want, you fools!' he muttered, slapping his thigh. 'Drive on, Leonid! It's not our car they're smashing up! Ha ha!' The butler, a nervous driver at the best of times, was less amused.

They pulled up on Tenth Rozhdestvenskaya, a narrow street of tall new apartment blocks. Gideon leaped out of the car, tugging his coat with its beaver collar around his shoulders.

'I'll be off then,' said Leonid.

'Hmm,' said Gideon, who had promised his wife,

children and brother Samuil to spend some time at home. But he could not quite commit himself. 'I'd like you to wait.'

'Sorry, Gospodin Zeitlin, I don't like to leave the car out for too long,' replied the servant. 'The Baron said, "Drop him off and come home," and I work for the baron. Besides, the motor car could get stoned by the workers and this is a beautiful machine, Gospodin Zeitlin, many times more beautiful than the Delaunay or—'

'Goodnight, Leonid, godspeed!'

Nodding cheerily at the doorman (while thinking, *you informing Okhrana scum!*), Gideon strolled through the marble lobby and caught the lift, an art-deco beauty of polished amber brass and black carving, to the fifth floor. The cognac and champagne he had drunk with Samuil rollicked through his body, making his heart burn, his bowels churn and his head spin. His wife Vera, mother of his two daughters, was pregnant again and he had spent all his meagre earnings on dinner at Contant's and games of chance. Oh, the tragedy, he chuckled to himself, of being born rich and growing up poor!

Once again his brother had bailed him out, opening his handsome teak strongbox to hand over the *mazuma* in two fresh green Imperial notes. But this time the baron had insisted he would not be opening it again for a long time.

'Oh, there he is!' said Vera, who was at the stove, in a shabby house-coat and slippers.

'That's a fine welcome for a returning prodigal,'

said Gideon, kissing her sallow cheek. 'Me? Of all people!' Despite his bad behaviour, Gideon was always amazed at how people treated him. He placed a colossal, hairy hand on her belly. 'How are you feeling, Commander-in-Chief?'

How firm and tight and tidy and full of life her belly feels, he thought. It's mine, the fruit of my seed – but who am I to bring another child into this pantomime of a life? The earth is spinning out of control . . .

Vera's strained voice softened. 'Good to see you, dear.'

'And you, and you!'

Then her weary face hardened again. 'Are you eating with us? How long are we to be honoured with your company, Gideon?'

'I'm here for you and the children,' answered Gideon so sunnily that anyone who did not know him would be convinced he was the best husband in Piter. Here, no one helped with his fur or galoshes. The apartment was messy and smelt of fat and cabbage, like a peasant's place. Like many disorderly men who never tidy up anything, Gideon hated mess and he inspected the unwashed dishes, the unmade beds with their yellowed sheets, the piles of shoes and boots, the footmarks on the carpets and the crumbs on the kitchen table with accusatory fury. It was a handsome apartment, painted plain white with ordinary Finnish birch furniture, but the pictures were still not hung. 'This place is a sewer, Vera. A sewer!'

'Gideon! We don't have a kopek. We must pay the butcher twenty roubles or we lose our credit. We owe the doorman eight, we owe—'

'Feh, feh, dearest. What's for dinner?'

'Kasha and cheese. We couldn't get anything else. There's nothing in the city to eat. Viktoria! Sophia! Your papa's here!'

There was the thud of reluctant feet in heavy lace-up shoes. A girl stood in the doorway, peering at her father with sullen, muddy eyes as if he was a Martian.

'Hello, Papa,' said Viktoria, known as Vika.

'Darling Vika! How are you! How's school? And that admirer of yours? Still writing you poems?'

He held open his arms but his darling fifteen-year-old daughter neither approached nor altered her expression.

'Mama's very tired. She cries. You haven't visited for a long time. We need money.'

Tall, olive-skinned with lanky hair, wearing horn-rimmed spectacles and a dressing gown, Vika reminded Gideon of a censorious librarian. He could not get close to her.

'Where have you been?' the girl went on. 'Drinking? Chasing women of easy virtue?'

'What a thing to accuse me of! Me? Of all people!' Gideon's eyes fell. Even though his big mouth, dancing black eyes, wild hair and beard were made for grand gestures and belly laughs, he felt hollow and ashamed. Where did she get such a phrase as

221

'women of easy virtue'? From that mother of hers of course.

'I've got homework to do,' said Vika, slouching away.

Gideon shrugged to himself: Vera was poisoning the children against him. Then he heard a cascade of light steps. Sophia, a dark girl with frizzy jet-black hair and eyes, threw herself into his arms. He stood up and whirled her round and round in her shabby nightshirt.

'Mouche!' he bellowed. 'My darling Mouche!' That was Sophia's nickname because when she was a baby she had resembled a mischievous fly. Now she was older, with black curls, black eyes and a strong jaw, she radiated energy just like her father.

'Where've you been? Is there a revolution? We saw a fight at the bakery! I want to be out there, Papa. Take me with you! How are your revolutionary friends? Did you see anything? I support the workers! How are you, Papa? Are you writing something? I've missed you. You haven't been bad, have you? We hope not! We are very prissy here!' She wrapped herself around him like a monkey. 'What are you writing, you old papa *momzer*?'

He loved the way she called him 'papa scallywag' in Yiddish and tickled his beard. 'Shall we write something now, Mouche? I owe them a quick article.'

'Oh yes!' Mouche took his hand and dragged him into the study, where it was difficult to step without knocking over piles of papers and journals – yet the fleet Mouche dodged them all and pulled out his green leather chair, adeptly placed the paper on the typewriter and wound it into position.

'*Pravilno!* Right!' he said.

'Now, who are we writing for today? The Kadets? The Mensheviks?'

'The Mensheviks!' he replied.

'So you're a Social Democrat this week?' she teased her father.

'This week!' He laughed at himself.

'How many words?'

'Five hundred, no more. Do we have something to drink?'

Mouche scurried off to get a thimble of vodka.

He swigged it and sat down in the chair.

Mouche settled into his lap, rested her hands on his arms and cried out: 'Type, Papa, begin! How about this? "The regime's reactionary follies are almost played out." Or "In the streets, I saw a hungry wraith of a woman, a worker's widow, shake her baby at a rich war profiteer." Or . . .'

'You're so like me,' he said, kissing her forehead.

Gideon was one of those journalists who, in a few minutes, could dash off an article decorated with ringing phrases and sharp reportage, without any real effort. Since he could never quite make up his mind whether he was a Constitutional Liberal – a Kadet – or a moderate Social Democrat, a Menshevik, he wrote for both their newspapers and several other journals, using different names. He had travelled widely and his pieces contained references to foreign cities and forgotten wars that impressed the reader. His phrases, so carelessly constructed, often hit home. People repeated them. Editors asked for more. He never regretted that he had let Samuil buy him out of the family business, though if he had kept his share he would now be a very rich man. He regretted nothing. Besides, money never stuck to his fingers.

He had promised the Menshevik editor a rousing article that evening on the atmosphere in the streets. Now, with Mouche excitedly feeling the tendons in his brawny arms as he typed, he worked fast, fingers banging into the keys and crying out, 'Return!' at the end of each line. Then Mouche returned the typewriter to begin another line, humming to herself with enjoyment, jiggling her knees with nervous energy.

'There,' he said. 'Done. Your papa's just earned himself a few roubles for that.'

'Which we never see!' said Vera from the doorway.

'I might just surprise you this time!' Gideon was feeling virtuous. He had enough cash to pay off the debts, satisfy Vera, buy the girls new books and dresses, and some fine meals. He looked forward to handing over the *mazuma*: Vera would smile at him; Mouche would dance; even Vika would love him again.

When Vera served the kasha, a buckwheat porridge, sprinkled with goat's cheese, she again asked about the money, not mentioning there was a revolution afoot. Outside, the factory sirens started to blare and whine; a shot, more shots and then a barrage rang out; stolen cars raced down the streets, skidding, grinding their gears as peasants enjoyed their first driving lessons.

'Is Sashenka really a Bolshevik, Papa? How's Aunt Ariadna? Is it true the doctor prescribed her opium?' Mouche asked questions and hummed to herself as he tried to answer them. Vika glared at her father each time her mother pressed her lips together, sighed or sniffed sanctimoniously.

No one could ruin a meal for Gideon. Whether it was kasha in his dreary apartment or a sturgeon steak at the Contant, he was a vigorous trencherman, recounting the family news, smacking his lips, sniffing the nosh like a happy dog and soiling his beard without the slightest embarrassment.

'You don't eat as you taught us to eat,' said Vika. 'Your manners are terrible, aren't they, Mama?'

'Don't do as I do,' replied Gideon. 'Do as I say!'

'How can you tell the children that?' asked his wife.

'It's hypocrisy,' said Vika.

'You two are a regular trade union of sulking women! Cheer up,' said Gideon, putting his feet up on a filthy chair, already marked by his boots on other occasions.

'No more jokes, Gideon,' said Vera, sending Vika and Mouche to do their homework.

The moment he was alone with Vera, everything changed. Her drawn sallow face, made for martyrdom, irritated him. She was always wiping her nose with a green-stained rag. Her prissiness maddened him. He adored his daughters – or rather he adored Mouche – but what had happened to Vera? A child of the provincial bourgeois, the daughter of a Mariupol schoolteacher, she had been educated, an intellectual who worked on the literary journal *Apollo*, full of vim and enthusiasm, with a high bosom, blue eyes and golden hair. Now the bosom hung around her waist like udders, the eyes were watered down to a tepid pallor, and the hair was greying. How he had been so foolish as to get her pregnant again, he could barely believe! But on Mouche's birthday he had been overcome with a sort of erotic nostalgia for how she had been, forgetting how she was now. The fact that he himself had done this to her and that he felt guilty about it made him resent her all the more.

Only Mouche delighted him, and he decided that when she was a little older he would invite her to live with him. As for now, he could hardly stand it here another moment. Great events were taking shape on the streets; parties were throbbing in the hotels; a writer must see history being made; and he was stuck here with this strait-laced harridan.

Vera droned on with her complaints: the morning sickness was gone but her back ached and she could not sleep. The doorman made comments about Gideon's carryings-on. Vika had told her friends that her father was a revolutionary and a drunkard; Mouche was insubordinate and rude, the teachers complained about her, and she was growing out of all her boots and dresses. But there was no money; it was hard to get meat in the shops and impossible to find bread; the neighbours had heard from someone else in the block that Gideon had been seen drunk in the early hours in the Europa Hotel; and how did he think *that* made her feel?

A full belly never made Gideon sleepy; it went straight to his loins. It fortified his libido. For some reason, he cast his mind back to the lunch last week at his brother's house. The Lorises were famous for their happy marriage but the boring count was not at the lunch so Gideon had given Missy what he called the Gideon Manifesto: let us pleasure ourselves now for life is short and tomorrow we die. (Obvious as it was, the manifesto was surprisingly successful!) Now Gideon recalled how, as he was saying goodbye to Missy, she had looked into his face with her crinkly, twinkling eyes – her laughter making creases around them – and squeezed his hand unmistakably, saying, 'It would be wonderful to talk more about Meyerhold and the new theatre. I suppose you won't be at Baroness Rozen's at the Astoria on . . .'

and she named a date. It happened that it was tonight. Gideon had neglected to follow up – but now his refreshed and well-fed phallus, a brilliant interpreter of female intentions, stirred. He had to get to that party right away.

Missy had never paid him the slightest attention. She was worldly enough – she had to be open-minded to be friends with Ariadna. But she had never really flirted with anyone and certainly not with him. Gideon reflected that the war, the loss of respect, the ever-changing ministers and the disturbances on the streets must be shaking free some ripe fruit that would never otherwise have fallen to the ground. He thought about Missy Loris's body – that bobbed blonde was skinny and had no bosom – yet he suddenly hungered for the sheer unadulterated joy of tasting new skin, lips, the satin of her inner thighs. He smiled to himself: this ursine giant was capable of Herculean erotic feats that no one – except the women themselves – would have believed possible. He proposed the most deliciously outré acts of lovemaking in delicate French phrases that liberated the restraint of chorus girls and countesses alike. Yet he had never become complacent about this erotic success. Why did these lovely *bubelehs*, these babes, choose me? he thought. Me? Of all people! I'm an ugly brute – like a Jewish innkeeper! But what the hell, I'm not complaining!

He just could not help himself: he had to find Missy right away that night. But if he handed over the two hundred roubles to Vera now, he would have nothing to buy the ladies drinks and snacks. What to do? He groaned. He'd do what he always did.

Moments later, as Vera washed up morosely, Gideon fled, leaving fifty roubles on the hall table and keeping the rest for himself. Mouche helped him pull on his felt boots and handed him 'our Menshevik article!' while Vika shook her head, pursing her lips.

'You're leaving already, Papa? I knew it. I knew it. I knew it!'

'We'll change the locks, you deadbeat!' shouted Vera, but he was gone.

Outside in the streets, Gideon could not find a sleigh. As for Vera, the whiner would manage, he thought. Vera and Vika: what a pair of sourpusses! I'm a coward, an incorrigible shameful hedonist – but I'm so happy! Dizzy with anticipation! What's wrong with happiness? We make our own lives! What are humans? We're just animals. I'll die young. I won't make old bones so I'm just doing what my species does. Besides, I had to go! I have an article to deliver to the newspaper.

He smelt the icy air. Strange sounds echoed in the distance. Gunshots crackled, factory whistles sang, engines revved and screeched, voices chanted – but here all seemed oddly quiet. But as he strode towards the Astoria Hotel, his mind racing with the anticipation of Missy's bare shoulders, her soft belly, her smells of female sweat and scent, he stepped out into the wider streets. It started as a murmur, became a throbbing and grew into a roar. The broad boulevards were filling with masses of people, their covered heads and heavy coats making padded bundles of them as if they were automata all marching in the same direction.

Gideon weaved in and out, sometimes letting the current carry him, sometimes standing aside and watching them pass. He was excited. As a writer, he was witnessing something. But where was the army, the Cossacks?

He stepped into the hotel, home again among its gleaming parquet floors, the shiny gold and black lifts, the dark oak bar.

'The usual, Monsieur Zeitlin?' asked Roustam the barman. Inside the Astoria, the polished formality had given way to a wild and carefree holiday. Tossing his coat and hat at the hat-check girl and forgetting to remove his boots, Gideon padded towards the private room where Baroness Rozen was holding a soirée. A girl in a backless orange dress, a feather boa and yellow shoes – what Vera called a woman of easy virtue, but what Gideon affectionately called a *bubeleh* – hailed him like an old friend, and he beamed at her. She was holding a drink and offering him a sip. The receptionists laughed at her: were they drunk too? A couple, an officer and what appeared to be a respectable lady wearing a double rope of pearls,

230

sat kissing on the sofa in the foyer as if they were in a *kabinet*, not a public place. A doorman opened the double doors to the party and Gideon noticed that the red-faced servant did not bow, just smirked as if he knew what was inside Gideon's head.

Gideon almost fell into the room, pushing through uniforms and shoulderboards, frock coats and gowns, hearing them discussing the situation in the streets – until he saw a helmet of blonde hair, some pale shoulders and a long gloved arm with a gold-tipped cigarette and the smoke curling round above it like a snake from a basket.

'So you came,' Missy Loris said in her American accent.

'Was I meant to?'

Her smile raised those comely laughter dimples in her cheeks. 'Gideon, what's happening out there?'

He put his lips to her little high-set ear. 'We could all die tonight, *bubeleh*! What shall we do in our last moments?' It was one of his favourite lines from the Gideon Manifesto, and any moment now it was going to work.

CHAPTER 32

There were no cabs at the Finland Station when Sashenka arrived back in the city. There was hardly anyone on the train except for two old ladies, probably retired teachers, who were earnestly discussing whether the *Thirty Abominations*, a lesbian novel from before the war, by Lidia Zinovieva-Annibal, was a classic exposition of female sensuality or a disgusting unchristian potboiler.

The argument started politely enough but as the train pulled into the Finland Station the two ladies were shouting at each other, even cursing. 'You philistine, Olesya Mikhailovna, it's pornography plain and simple!'

'You hidebound reptile, Marfa Constantinovna, you've never lived, never loved, felt nothing.'

'At least I feared God!'

'You've so upset me, I'm having a turn. I need my pills.'

'I won't give them to you until you admit you're being utterly unreasonable . . .'

Sashenka could only smile as she heard the ricochet of gunshots over the city.

The station was eerily empty of its tramps and urchins. Outside, it was dusk but the streets were filled with running people, some with guns. It was snowing again, big dry flakes like barley seeds; the half-moon cast a lurid yellow light. Sashenka thought the people looked oddly swollen but realized that many were wearing two coats or padding to fend off the knouts of the Cossacks. A worker from one of the vast metal factories told her there was a stand-off at the Alexander Bridge, but before she could ask any more there was shooting and everyone began to run, unsure what they were running from. A female worker from the Putilov Works told her there had been battles on Alexander Bridge and Znamenskaya Square; that some of the Cossacks, the Volynsky Guards, had changed sides and charged the police. An old drunk claimed he was a socialist but then tried to put his hand into Sashenka's coat. He squeezed her breast and she slapped him and then ran. On the Alexander Bridge, she thought she saw the bodies of policemen. There were no trams.

She walked slowly towards home down the famous avenues, now seething with dark figures. Bonfires were lit in the streets. Urchins danced around the flames like demonic gnomes. An arsenal had been stormed: workers now carried rifles. She tramped onwards, exhausted yet vibrating with fear and excitement. Whatever Uncle Mendel claimed about the Revolution, the people had not melted away at the first sign of

233

resistance. There was the crackle of more shooting. Two boys, young workers, kissed her on both cheeks and ran on.

She came upon a crowd of soldiers on Nevsky. 'Brothers, sisters, daughters, mothers, I propose that we don't fire on our brethren,' shouted some NCO to cries of 'Hurrah! Down with the autocracy!' She tried to find her comrades but they were at none of the coachmen's cafés or the safehouses on Nevsky.

Hurrying on, Sashenka felt wildly joyful. Was this it? A revolution without leaders? Where were the machine-gun nests and Cossacks and pharaohs? She heard a roaring engine. The people in the streets froze and watched, raising white faces like moons: what could it be? Like a dinosaur, a grey Austin armoured car mounted with a howitzer drove haphazardly, gears screaming, in random accelerations and jerking turns, down Nevsky. The crowd scattered as it mounted the pavement and drove straight over a bonfire outside Yeliseyev's grocery store, and then stopped beside a group of soldiers.

'Can anyone drive this thing?' shouted the driver.

'I can!' A young man with shaggy black hair and bright brown eyes jumped up. 'I learned in the army.' It was her comrade Vanya Palitsyn, the Bolshevik metal worker. Sashenka hurried towards him to ask for instructions but he was already inside the armoured car, which revved, shook then accelerated off down the Prospect.

'Are you for the Revolution?' asked a stranger, a boy with a Ukrainian accent, a blue nose and a military jacket. It was the first time anyone had used that word.

'I'm a Bolshevik!' Sashenka said proudly. They hugged spontaneously. Soon she was asking the question herself. Strangers embraced around her: a grizzled sergeant-major, a Polish student, a fat woman wearing an apron under her sheepskin, a leather-clad metal worker in a tool belt, even a fashionable woman in a seal coat. Closer to home, cars filled with soldiers waving banners and rifles skidded down Nevsky and Greater Maritime.

Dizzy with the momentum of this chaotic night, Sashenka kept thinking of Sagan. She was keen to make her report to Mendel. She had got the name of the traitor, established Sagan as a Bolshevik source inside the Okhrana, and was now a fully fledged practitioner of the art of conspiracy. She could hand over the direction of their double agent to another comrade. The mission was over, and away from Sagan and the effect he had on her, she was relieved. The Party would be satisfied.

She racked her brain for other Party safehouses. She tried 106 Nevsky. No answer. Then 134. The door was open. She flung herself upstairs, her senses bristling. The door was just opening and she could hear the Jericho trumpet of Mendel's voice. 'What are we doing?' he was shouting.

'I just don't know,' replied Shlyapnikov, wearing a padded greatcoat. 'I'm not sure . . .'

'Let's go to G-g-gorky's apartment,' suggested Molotov, rubbing his bulging forehead. 'He'll know something . . .'

Shlyapnikov nodded and headed for the door.

'This is it,' she said. Her voice squeaked, not her own. 'The Revolution.'

'Don't lecture the committee, comrade,' answered Shlyapnikov as he and Molotov clumped down the stairs. 'You're a puppy.'

Mendel lingered for a moment.

'Who's in charge?' asked Sashenka. 'Where's Comrade Lenin? Who's in charge?'

'We are!' Mendel smiled suddenly. 'Lenin's in Geneva. We are the Party leadership.'

'I met Sagan,' she whispered. 'Verezin the Horse Guards concierge is the traitor. But I don't suppose it matters any more . . .'

'C-c-comrade!' called Molotov from the lobby, stammer reverberating up the stairs.

'I've got to go,' said Mendel. 'Check the other apartments for comrades. There's a meeting at the Taurida Palace. Tell them to report there later.'

Mendel limped down the stairs, leaving Sashenka alone.

She returned to Nevsky, heading home. She ate some *solianka* soup and a chunk of black Borodinsky bread at the carriage-drivers' café, which was full of workers and coachmen, each telling stories of mayhem, orgies, slaughter, hunger and treason in loud, tipsy voices without listening to anyone else. Coal and oat prices had quadrupled. Even a bowl of soup in the café had gone up seven times. There were German agents, Jewish traitors and crooks everywhere.

As Sashenka put some coins into the barrel organ, which incongruously played 'God Save the Tsar', raising guffaws from the coachmen, the streets grew darker. There were distant sounds like lions coughing in the night, the groan grew into a deafening roar and the hut shook. At first she could not understand why – then she realized that as she had been eating, the coachmen's café had been surrounded, overrun by a sea of people in dark coats. They were blocking the streets. There was shooting in the distance and smoke rising, pink against the pale darkness: the Kresty Prison was on fire.

As she walked down Greater Maritime, Sashenka saw a soldier and a girl kissing against a wall. She could not see their faces but the man groped up the girl's skirt past her stocking tops while the girl tore open his fly buttons. A leg rose up his side like one of the Neva's bridges opening. The girl mewed and writhed. Sashenka thought of Sagan and the sleigh ride in the snowfields and hurried on.

Outside the Astoria, some soldiers were stealing a Rolls-Royce, punching a uniformed chauffeur. The doorman, an officer and a gendarme ran outside, shouting. The soldiers calmly shot the officer and the gendarme, and the car drove off with its horn blowing.

Presently, a bearded man staggered heartily past her singing '*Nightingale, nightingale*' with a blonde woman in a fur coat and Sashenka recognized Gideon and Countess Loris. She was relieved to find friends and was about to hail them when Gideon cupped Missy's buttocks and pulled her out of the crowd and into a doorway where they started kissing frenziedly.

A volley of shots distracted Sashenka. Figures were climbing up the facade of the Mariinsky Palace and tearing down the double-headed eagle of the Romanovs.

The gendarme's body lay in the street, splayed so that his white belly bulged out of his trousers, like a dead fish. Exhausted beyond belief, Sashenka stepped over it and hurried down Nevsky – towards the Taurida Palace.

CHAPTER 33

'What are you all standing around for?' Ariadna called from the top of the stairs, her hair up, elegant in a flounced dress of shantung silk. The faces of Leonid the butler, the two chauffeurs and the parlourmaids were raised towards her as she started to descend.

'Haven't you heard, Baroness?' It was Pantameilion, always the cheekiest, his neat moustache, oiled hair and sharp chin thrusting impertinently.

'Heard what? Speak up!'

'They've formed a Workers' Soviet at the Taurida Palace,' he said excitedly, 'and we've heard that—'

'That's yesterday's news,' snapped Ariadna. 'Please get on with your work.'

'And the crowds say . . . the Tsar's abdicated!' said Pantameilion.

'Rubbish! Stop spreading rumours, Pantameilion. Go and decarbonize the car,' replied Ariadna. 'The baron would know if anyone did – he's at the Taurida!'

At that moment, the front door opened and Zeitlin swept in, a commanding figure in his floor-length black coat with a beaver collar and *shapka*. Ariadna and the servants stared open-mouthed as if he alone could settle the great question of the epoch.

Zeitlin cheerfully tossed his hat at the stand. He appeared years younger, radiating confidence. So there! thought Ariadna, the Tsar is back in control. What nonsense the servants talk! Fools! Peasants!

Zeitlin leaned on his cane and looked up at Ariadna like a tenor about to sing an Italian aria.

'I have news,' he said in a voice quivering with excitement.

There! The Cossacks are guarding the streets, the Germans are retreating, everything will settle down again as it always does, decided Ariadna. Long live the Emperor!

On cue, Lala came down the stairs, Shifra emerged from the Black Way and Delphine the cook from the kitchen, her customary drip dangling from the end of her nose.

'The Emperor has abdicated,' announced Zeitlin. 'First in favour of the Tsarevich then in favour of his brother Grand Duke Michael. Prince Lvov has formed a government. All political parties are now legal. That's it! We're entering a new era!'

'The Tsar gone!' Leonid crossed himself then started to sob. 'Our little father – abdicated!'

Pantameilion grinned insolently, twisting his moustache and whistling through his teeth. The two parlourmaids paled.

'Woe is me!' Shifra whispered. 'Thrones tumble like in the Book of Revelation!'

'What next? George V?' said Lala. 'What'll become of me here?'

Delphine started to weep and her perpetual drip separated itself from the cosy berth of her nostrils and fell to the floor. The household had waited twenty years for this historic event but now that it had happened, no one noticed.

'Come on, Leonid,' said Zeitlin, offering the butler his silk handkerchief, a gesture which, Ariadna noted, he would never have made a week earlier. 'Pull yourselves together. Nothing changes in my house. Take my coat. What time is lunch, Cook? I'm ravenous.'

Ariadna gripped the marble banisters, watching the servants pull off Zeitlin's boots. The Emperor was gone. She had grown up with Nicholas II and suddenly felt quite rootless.

Zeitlin leaped up the stairs, taking two at a time, like a young man. Following her into her bedroom, he kissed her on the lips so energetically that it made her head spin and then talked about the new Russia. The crowds were still out of control. The police headquarters were burning; policemen and informers were being killed; soldiers and bandits were driving automobiles and armoured cars around the streets, shooting their rifles in the air. The former Emperor wanted to return to Tsarskoe Selo but was now under arrest, soon to be reunited with his wife and children – they would not be harmed. Grand Duke Michael would turn down the throne.

Zeitlin was elated, he told his wife, because many of his friends from the Kadets and Octobrists were serving in Prince Lvov's government. The war would go on; he had already been commissioned by the new War Minister to deliver more rifles and howitzers; and it turned out that Sashenka was still a Bolshevik. He had seen her at the Taurida Palace with her comrades – a motley bunch of fanatics – but youth will be youth.

'There, you see, Ariadna? We're a republic. Russia's a sort of democracy!'

'What will happen to the Tsar?' asked Ariadna, feeling dazed. 'What will happen to us?'

'What do you mean?' replied Zeitlin affably. 'There'll be changes of course. The Poles and Finns want independence, but we'll be fine. There are opportunities in all this. In fact, when I was in the Taurida, I had a word with . . .'

Ariadna barely noticed when Zeitlin, still babbling about new ministers and juicy contracts, checked his gold fob watch and went downstairs to his office to make telephone calls. Almost in a trance, she followed him out of her room and watched him descend. She heard the Trotting Chair rumble into action.

Leonid rushed to the front door. Sashenka came into the hall, pale and elated, dressed in that plain blouse and grey skirt, her hair in an ugly bun, and no rouge at all. Ariadna was disappointed in her daughter: why did she dress like a provincial schoolteacher? What a sight the child was! She stank too, of smoke, soup kitchens and the people, the rushing gadding people. Even a Bolshevik needed to use powder and lipstick, and why did she refuse to wear her new dresses from Chernyshev's? A decent dress would improve her no end.

But somehow Sashenka was utterly triumphant, glowing even. 'Hello, Mama!' she called up but then, throwing off her fur *shuba* and boots, she swept on to answer the questions of Lala and the servants. Excitedly, Sashenka told them that the Soviet of Workers and Soldiers was sitting; that Uncle Mendel was on the Executive Committee. And that Uncle Gideon was there too – he was writing about it – and his friends, the Mensheviks, dominated the Soviet.

Ariadna did not care about this politicking but she could see that Sashenka needed to sleep. Her eyes were red, her hands shook from coffee and exhilaration. Yet as she watched her daughter's animated face, she saw Sashenka anew. It was as if she had grown strong and beautiful, like a grub eating her mother's flesh from the inside. Now she was shining with life while Ariadna was lifeless and empty.

Stifling a longing to weep, Ariadna retreated to her bedroom.

★　　★　　★

Feeling not so much calm as becalmed, Ariadna measured out Dr Gemp's opium tonic and swallowed it. But this time it did not work. Her limbs were heavy, as if moving through treacle. The earth seemed to slow down, almost stopping on its axis. Time became excruciating.

She lay down on her divan. She could not rejoice in the news that made her husband feel younger and her daughter seem beautiful, it merely aged her. The ground was splintering beneath her feet. No Tsar; Rasputin dead; Zeitlin had talked divorce; and somehow what most upset her was Sashenka's joyous luminosity. She was playing grown-up politics, laughing at her parents. She had a mission in life – but what did Ariadna have? Why was Sashenka happy? Why so smug? The clock ticked more and more slowly. She waited for each tick but it took ages to come and when it did, it was like the tolling of a distant bell.

When Ariadna was growing up in Turbin, she knew the Tsars were no friend of the Jews, but the Jews were convinced that without the Tsars it would be much worse. The Tsar was far away and he did much harm to the Jews and to the Russians too, even if his intentions were not too bad. But the Tsar had protected the Jews against the Cossacks, landowners, anti-Semites and pogromists. Now he was gone, who would protect them? Who would look after her? Suddenly she craved her mother's embrace, her mother whom she had ignored. Miriam was in the same house, so was her father – but they might have been in another universe. To reach them would take an eternity.

The sounds of the household were muffled. She had nothing to do and the nothingness took for ever to pass. The world was soaked in blood, just as Rasputin had warned her it would be; the streets of Piter were in anarchy. Outside, she heard tramping feet, hooting cars, cheering and gunfire. The sounds meant nothing; everything had lost its taste; her scent smelt of dust. Everything, even her scarlet dresses, her sapphires, looked grey.

She rose with a sigh and wandered towards Sashenka's room. She realized that she had not visited it for years.

CHAPTER 34

Baron Zeitlin was in his study, clanking energetically on his Trotting Chair, a cigar between his teeth. He was sure he could adapt to the new world, indeed he almost sympathized with the socialists. He was vibrating with new plans. Then he heard Sashenka's voice in the lobby and remembered how he had failed to understand her. Now he must try harder – otherwise he would lose her.

'Darling Sashenka!' She burst in breathlessly but did not sit down. 'I can't believe the last few days. But life must go on. When are you starting your studies?'

'Studies? We're much too busy for studies. I lied to you about my politics, Papa, because I had to. We Bolsheviks live by special rules. I was doing what was right.' Her face was firm, almost aggressive.

'It's all right, Sashenka, I understand,' said Zeitlin, but he did not. He blamed himself for making his daughter into this godless avenger. She had lied to him and rejected the family. But he had taught her to disrespect faith and this was the result. And now was not the time for another row. 'Your mother thought you had a boyfriend.'

'How absurd! She hardly knows me. I have a job now at the *Pravda* newspaper as liaison with the Petrograd Committee and the Soviet.'

'But you must go back to school. The Revolution's almost over, Sashenka. The government . . .'

'Papa, the Revolution's just started. There are exploiters and exploited. No middle ground. This government's just a temporary bourgeois stage in the march to Socialism. The peasants must have their land, the workers their equality. The soldiers now take their orders from the Soviet of Workers' and Soldiers' Deputies.' She was almost shouting at him now, flushed with defiance, her hands gripping his arms. 'There'll be one last stage of capitalist corruption and then all this rottenness, all the bloodsuckers – yes, even you, Papa – will be swept away. There'll be blood on the streets. I love you, Papa, but we Bolsheviks don't have families and my love counts for nothing in the face of history.'

Zeitlin had stopped trotting on his contraption. He looked at his daughter, at her exquisite freckles and dappled eyes, and was stunned.

Silence. From somewhere else in the house, there was a small pop.

'Did you hear that?' said Zeitlin, taking his cigar out of his mouth. 'What was it?'

'It might have come from upstairs.'

Father and daughter went out into the hall and then, for some reason, they were running. Leonid was at the top of the stairs, Lala on the landing. All were looking at the door of Ariadna's room. A cold hand clutched his heart, and Zeitlin rushed up the stairs.

'Ariadna!' he shouted, knocking on the door. The staff peered past him, goggle-eyed.

Ariadna was snowily naked on the divan. The smoking Mauser, dark and chunky, rested on her stomach. On her white skin, blood dripped crimson down her breast and pooled on the floor.

CHAPTER 35

Sashenka stood at the window of the Gogol Street safehouse, not far from the War Ministry, smoking a cigarette and peering out over the frozen Neva at the Peter and Paul Fortress. It was dark, yet the sky glowed an unnatural purple like a theatrical screen with a light behind it. The lantern atop the spire of the fortress's church swung a little in the wind.

The workers controlled the fortress. Mendel and Trotsky had once been prisoners in the Trubetskoy Bastion but yesterday the prisoners had all been freed. It was early evening and the streets were still teeming as jovial crowds tore down any remaining Romanov eagles. The Okhrana headquarters was on fire.

Sashenka's dreams were coming true but now she was numb. She walked the streets without seeing or hearing the remarkable sights. Her mother had pulled off the impossible: she had upstaged the Russian Revolution. People bumped into Sashenka. Someone embraced her. Vanya Palitsyn called her name from a careering car filled with Red Guards, a Romanov crest on its doors.

The apartment was too hot; she was sweating because she had not taken off her coat or hat. Why on earth had she walked straight here again? A place she had promised never to revisit. She had tried to block Sagan out of her mind; his time was past and probably he was already in Stockholm or the south. Yet here she was, in the familiar apartment, waiting for the person she was accustomed to confiding in about her mother.

She heard a sound and turned slowly. Captain Sagan, still in full gendarme uniform but haggard and bleary, stood there pointing a Walther pistol at her. Suddenly he looked his age, older even.

They said nothing for a moment. Then he put the pistol back in its holster and without a word came to her. They hugged. She was grateful he was there.

'I've got some brandy,' he said, 'and the samovar's just boiled.'

'How long have you been here?'

'I came last night. I didn't know where else to come. Some workers went to my home and my wife has gone. The trains aren't running. I didn't know where to go so I just came here. Sashenka, I want to tell you something that will surprise you. My world – everything I cherished – has vanished in a night.'

'That's not what you told me would happen.'

'I'm in your hands. You can turn me in. I was a believer in the Empire. And yet I told you the truth about myself.'

He took a bottle of Armenian brandy, cheap *cha-cha*, and poured out two shots, handing one to Sashenka. He downed his. She took off her coat and hat.

'Why are you here?' he asked. 'I'd have thought you'd be celebrating.'

'I was. And then something terrible happened. I was going to the Taurida Palace but when I passed the guardhouse at the barracks I knocked on the door. It was open. The doorman – remember the doorman, Verezin? – was lying dead on the floor, shot in the head. And then I went into the Soviet and met my comrades.'

'You'd told them he was a traitor?'

She nodded.

'And you were surprised that he was dead?'

'No, I wasn't surprised. A bit shocked, I suppose. But that's revolution for you. When you chop wood, chips fly.'

'But you said something terrible had happened?'

'My mother shot herself.'

Sagan was aghast. 'I'm so sorry, Sashenka. Is she dead?'

'No, she is just about alive. She shot herself in the chest. Apparently, beautiful women tend to avoid their faces. She found my Mauser, the Party's Mauser, under my mattress. How did she know it was there? How could she have found it? The doctors are there now.' Sashenka paused, struggling to control her breathing. 'I should have gone to the newspaper but instead I found myself

251

here. Because it was here . . . with you . . . that we talked so much about her. I hated her. I never told her how much . . .'

She started to cry and Sagan put his arms around her. His hair smelt of smoke, his neck almost tasted of cognac, yet she found that just telling Sagan about her mother had calmed her. His hug restored her and, ironically, gave her the strength to pull away.

'Sashenka,' he said, his hands squeezing her shoulders, 'I have something to tell you. I was doing my job but I never told you how much I came to . . . be fond of you. I have no one else. I . . .'

She went cold suddenly.

'You're so much younger than me but I think I love you.'

Sashenka stepped backwards. She knew she had needed him, but not as the man who had kissed her in the snowfields, more as a confidant. Now his need for her, his stench of desperation, repelled her, and this spectre of the fallen regime was frightening her. She wanted to be away from him.

'You can't just leave me like that,' he cried, 'after what I just told you.'

'I never asked for this, never.'

'You can't leave . . .'

'I've got to go,' she said and, sensing a change in him, rushed for the door. He was right behind her.

He grabbed her around the waist and pulled her

back to the divan, where she had sat so many nights talking of poetry and parents.

She punched his jaw. 'Let me go,' she screamed. 'What are you doing?'

But he seized her hands and pushed her down, his face terrifyingly close, his long thin face pouring sweat and dribbling saliva as he struggled with her. He thrust his other hand up her skirt, tearing her stockings, driving up between her thighs. Then he turned to her chest, ripping the buttons off her blouse, rending her undergarments and clawing at her breasts.

She twisted sharply, freed her hands and smacked him in the nose. His blood burst all over her face but his weight held her down. Then she pulled the Walther out of his holster and slammed it sideways into his face. She felt the steel connect with teeth, bone and flesh, and more blood oozed over her fingers.

He rolled off her, and she was on her feet and racing for the door. As she wrenched it open, she glimpsed him curled like a child on the divan, sobbing.

Sashenka did not stop until she was downstairs and out of the building. She hurtled into a cellar bar full of drunken soldiers but they were shocked by the sight of her and, seizing their bayoneted rifles, offered their help in killing anyone who had laid a finger on her. In the bathroom she washed the blood off her face and buttoned her blouse. The metallic taste of Sagan's blood was in her mouth, nose, everywhere, and she tried to wash it away but the smell made her gag, and she vomited. When she came out, she took a vodka from one of the soldiers and drank it down. It cleansed her a little, and gradually she felt calmer.

Outside, the streets were still heaving. She heard a burst of shooting on Nevsky. They were lynching pickpockets, and there were drunken gangs of deserters and bandits on the loose. She sensed that Sagan would want to get away from the apartment, so she hid in a doorway and watched the exit from the block. Her head was throbbing, and the lingering taste of his blood made her retch again. Her body was shaking. This had all been for the Party, and now it was over. She told herself that she should feel a sense of triumph – for she had won the Superlative Game, Sagan and his masters were finished, and his attack on her reflected his humiliation. Yet all she could feel was a corrosive shame and a savage fury. She imagined returning with her Party pistol and shooting him as a police spy, but instead, fumbling, she lit up a Crocodile.

About half an hour later, Sagan came out into the street and, in the queer purple light of night, she saw his swollen, bleeding face, his broken gait, how diminished he was. He was just a crooked, lanky figure hunched beneath a high astrakhan hat, his uniform covered by a khaki greatcoat. The streets were seething with huddled men, armed with Berdanas and Mausers, staggering in padded coats. The night was balanced on that thin spine between chanting jubilation and growing ugliness. Sagan headed down Gogol, through the small streets, and across Nevsky. She followed and saw the workers surround him outside the Kazan Cathedral. Perhaps they'd give him a good beating and punish him for hurting her, she thought, but they let him through. Then he tripped on a paving stone and they saw his uniform.

'A gendarme! A pharaoh! Let's arrest him! Scum! Bastard! We'll take him to the Soviet! We'll throw him in the bastion! Here, take this on the smiler, you weasel!' They surrounded him, but he must have drawn his pistol. He got off a shot – there it was, that popping sound again. Then they were kicking at a bundle on the ground, jeering, shouting and raising their rifle butts and bayonets. Breathing raggedly, Sashenka watched it all happen too fast for her to really understand.

Somewhere inside the cacophony of blows and cries, she heard his voice and then the squealing of an animal in pain. The moist thudding of the rifle butts told the rest. Through the workers' boots and the skirts of their greatcoats, she could see blood glistening on the dark uniform. She did not see the metamorphosis of a man into a smeared heap on the street – and when it was over, there was a hush after the frenzy, as the crowd cleared their throats, straightened their clothes and then shuffled away. She did not wait any longer. She had seen the power of the people in action – the judgement of history.

Yet she no longer felt as if she had won. A wave of sadness and guilt overwhelmed her, as if her curse had visited this horror upon him. The dead body of Verezin, and now this. Yet *this* was what she had craved and she must welcome it: the Revolution was a noble master. Many would die in the struggle, she thought – and yet the destruction of a man was a terrible thing.

She found herself leaning on a statue outside the Kazan as tears ran down her face. It was an end but not the one she had wanted. She wished she had never known Sagan and she wished too that he had walked on down that street to a safe exile, far away.

CHAPTER 36

A husky drawl broke the sepulchral hush of the sickroom.

'What's in the newspaper?' Ariadna asked.

The familiar voice shocked Sashenka. Her mother had not spoken for days. She had just slept, her breathing laboured, the infection flourishing in her chest so that it seemed she would never wake again. Sashenka had been reading *Pravda*, the Party newspaper, when Ariadna stirred. She spoke so clearly that Sashenka dropped the paper, scattering its pages on to the carpet.

'Mama, you gave me a shock!'

'I'm not dead yet, darling . . . or am I? It stinks in here. I can hardly breathe. What does that newspaper say?'

Sashenka picked up the pages. 'Uncle Mendel's on the Party's Central Committee. Lenin's returning any day.' Sashenka looked up to find her mother's velvety eyes were resting on her with an astonishing warmth. It surprised and then embarrassed her.

'When I finally went to your room . . .' Ariadna began, and Sashenka strained to understand.

'Mama, you look better.' It was a lie but who tells the truth to the dying? Sashenka wanted to soothe her mother. 'You're getting better. Mama, how do you feel?'

'I feel . . .' She squeezed her daughter's hand. Sashenka squeezed back. The eyes dimmed again.

'I long to ask you one question, Mama. Why did you . . . ? Mama?'

At that moment Dr Gemp, a plump, worldly man with a shiny pink pate and the theatrical air often associated with society doctors, entered the room.

'Did your mother wake up then? What did she say?' he asked. 'Ariadna, are you in pain?'

Sashenka watched him lean over her mother, bathing her forehead and neck with a cold compress. He unravelled the dressing on her chest and inspected, cleaned and dabbed the wound, which looked like a congealed fist of blood.

Her father appeared beside her, also leaning over the sickbed. He looked terrible, his collar filthy and the beginnings of a prickly grey beard on his cheeks. He reminded Sashenka of an old Jew from the Pale.

'Is she coming round? Ariadna? Speak to me! I love you, Ariadna!' said Zeitlin. Ariadna opened her eyes. 'Ariadna! Why did you harm yourself? Why?'

Behind him stood Ariadna's parents, Miriam,

her small, dry face pointed like that of a field mouse, and the Rabbi of Turbin, with gaberdine coat and skullcap, his face framed by his prophetic beard and whimsical ringlets.

'Darling Silberkind,' said Miriam in her strong Polish-Yiddish accent, taking Sashenka's hands and kissing her shoulder tenderly. But Sashenka sensed how out of place the old couple felt in Ariadna's room. They had been in there before, yet they peered, like paupers, at the pearls, gowns, tarot cards and potions. For them this was the Temple of the Golden Calf and the very ruin of their dreams as parents.

Dr Gemp, who specialized in the secret tragedies – abortions, suicides and addictions – of Grand Dukes and counts, stared at the old Jews as if they were lepers, but managed to finish dressing Ariadna's wound.

Ariadna pointed at her parents. 'Are you from Turbin?' she asked them. 'I was born in Turbin. Samuil, you must shave . . .'

Hours, nights, days passed. Sashenka lost track of time as she sat by the bed. Ariadna's breathing was hoarse and laboured, like an old pair of bellows. Her face was grey and sallow and sunken. She had become old, tiny and collapsed. Her jaw hung open, and her chest creaked up and down, catching on clots of phlegm in her lungs so that her breath rattled and crackled. There was no beauty or vivacity left, just this shivering, quivering animal that had once been a vibrant woman, a mother, Sashenka's mother.

Sometimes Ariadna struggled to breathe, and began to panic. Sweat poured off her, soaking the sheets, and she clawed the bed. Then Sashenka would stand up and take her hand. All of a sudden, there was so much she wanted to say to her mother: she wanted to love her, wanted to be loved by her. Was it too late?

'Mama, I'm here with you, it's me, Sashenka! I love you, Mama!' Did she love her? She was not sure, but her voice was saying these things.

Dr Gemp came again. He pulled Zeitlin and Sashenka aside.

'Don't raise your hopes, Samuil,' said the doctor.

'But she wakes up sometimes! She talks . . .' said Zeitlin.

'The wound's infected and the infection has spread.'

'She could recover, she could . . .' insisted Sashenka.

'Perhaps, mademoiselle,' replied Dr Gemp smoothly, as a maid handed him his black cape and fedora. 'Perhaps in the land of miracles.'

CHAPTER 37

'Would you like me to read something to you?' Ariadna heard her daughter ask the next morning.

'No need,' she replied, 'because I can come and read it myself.' Another Ariadna rose up from the Ariadna on the bed and hovered over Sashenka's shoulder. She looked down and barely recognized the waxy creature with a dressing on her chest, breathing fast like a sick dog. Her hair was lank and greasy but she did not demand that Luda bring the curling tongs – so she *must* be dying. Ariadna wondered if she had always been cursed by the Evil Eye or infested by a dybbuk, or whether she had brought all her troubles upon herself.

She spun away from reality into wondrous dreams. She flew gracefully around the room. What visions she had! She and Samuil were together in a garden with tinkling fountains and luscious peaches. Were they in the Garden of Eden? No, the forests were slim silver birches: these were Zeitlin's forests, soon to be the butts of rifles in the dead hands of Russian solders. The birches turned into a crowd of people, all dancing.

The trees were ballerinas in tutus, then stark naked.

She opened her eyes. She was in her room again. Sashenka was sleeping on the divan. It was night. The room was softly lit by a lamp, not electric light. Samuil and two old Jews, a man and a woman, were talking quietly.

'I've lost myself, Rabbi,' said Samuil in Yiddish. 'I no longer know who I am. I'm not a Jew, not a Russian. I have long ago ceased to be a good husband or a good father. What should I do? Should I wear phylacteries and pray as a religious Jew, or should I become a socialist? I thought I had my life in order and now . . .'

'You're just a man, Samuil,' answered the bearded sage.

Ariadna knew that voice: it was her father. What a fine voice, so deep and kind. Would he curse Samuil and call him a heathen? she wondered.

'You've done bad things and good things. Like all of us,' her father said.

'So what should I do?'

'Do good. Do nothing bad.'

'It sounds simple.'

'It's very hard but it is a great thing. Don't harm yourself or others. Love your family. Ask for God's mercy.'

'But I'm not even sure I believe in him.'

'You do. Or you would not be asking these questions. All of us sin. The body is for sinning in this world. Without the choice, goodness would be meaningless. The soul is the bridge between this world and the next. But everything is God's world. Even for you, even for poor, darling Finkel, God's mercy is there, waiting. That is all you need to understand.'

Who on earth was Finkel? Ariadna asked herself. Of course, it was her real name. Her father and her bewigged mother seemed to her at one moment like laughable cartoons; at another, they were as sacred as priests in the Temple of Solomon.

'And Ariadna?' Samuil asked.

'A suicide.' Her father shook his head. Her mother started to weep.

'I blame myself,' said Samuil.

'You did more for her than us, more than anyone,' said her father. 'We failed her; she failed us. But we love her. God loves her.'

Ariadna was moved; she felt fondness for her parents, but not love. She no longer loved anyone. These were characters from her life, familiar faces and voices, but she loved none of them.

She was light as a goose feather, a draught from a window blew her this way and that. Her body lay there, croaking and wheezing. She was interested in this, but not involved in its mechanical functions. Dr Gemp came into the room and threw off his cape like a Spanish bullfighter. She felt her forehead being dabbed; her dressing changed; morphine injected; her lips wetted with warm, sugary tea. Her belly ached; bowels groaned; the congested fist in her chest throbbed around a single bullet that she herself had placed there. This thing on the bed – the body she recognized as hers – was no more important than a laddered pair of stockings, a good pair, silk from Paris, but an object that could be thrown away without a thought.

Her father was praying aloud, reading from the Psalms, singing in a deep chant that filled her with disinterested joy. It was the voice of a nightingale outside in the garden. But when she looked at his face, he was young, his beard a reddish-brown, eyes strong and bright. Her mother was there too, full of life, even younger. She did not wear a wig but her own long blonde hair in braids, and a girl's dress. And her grandparents too, all much younger than she. There was her husband as a teenager. Sashenka as a little girl. They could now be her sisters and brothers.

The rabbi's chanting carried her to Turbin three decades earlier. In the courtyard at Passover time in a cold year, her brothers Mendel and little Avigdor were throwing snowballs with some other boys outside the cheder, the Jewish schoolhouse, Avigdor energetic and mischievous yet already challenging and disrespectful of religious matters, Mendel, in gaberdine with yarmulke and ringlets, limping from the polio, intense, dutiful and religious, hailed as a scholar, a future rabbi.

Her father and the beadle were walking out of the studyhouse; her mother was cooking dumplings and noodles laced with saffron, cinnamon and cloves. Ariadna was in trouble even then: she had refused to marry the son of the Mogilevsky rabbi, had been seen talking to one of the Litvak lads who did not even wear ringlets – and she had met a Russian officer in the woods near the barracks. She adored that uniform, the gold buttons, the boots, the shoulderboards. No one knew she had kissed not only the Litvak boy but also the young Russian, sipping cognac that made her glow, their hands all over her, her skin fluttering under their caresses. How that officer must have boasted and laughed to his friends in the officers' mess: 'You'll never guess what I found in the woods today. A lovely Jewess fresh as the dew . . .'

I was too beautiful for the rabbi's court in Turbin, she told herself. I was a peacock in a stable. And now she was happily going back to Turbin. Or at least passing through there, on the way to somewhere else. What was written for her in the Book of Life? It suddenly seemed an important question, the most important of all.

But when Ariadna flew back to that familiar bedroom filled with family and re-entered her body, she realized that it was no longer her bedroom, Sashenka was no longer her daughter, Miriam no longer her mother – and she herself was no longer Ariadna Finkel Barmakid, Baroness Zeitlin. She became something else, and she was filled with joy.

Sashenka was the first to notice. 'Papa,' she said, 'look! Mama's smiling.'

CHAPTER 38

'She's gone,' said Miriam, taking her daughter's hand.

'Woe is to outlive your own child,' said the rabbi quietly and then he started to pray for his daughter. Sashenka felt that she had made some peace with her mother, but her father, who had been napping on the divan, awoke and threw himself on to the body, weeping.

Uncle Gideon, now writing for Gorky's *New Life* newspaper, flirting with both the Mensheviks and the Bolsheviks, was also there, waiting in the corridor, smelling of ladies' scent and cigars, and he rushed into the room and lifted Zeitlin off Ariadna's body. He was immensely strong and he carried the baron away and sat him in a chair outside.

The doctor sent them all out. He closed Ariadna's mouth and her eyes and then called them back. 'Come and see her now,' he instructed.

'She's become . . . beautiful again,' Sashenka whispered. 'Yet there's no one there.' Sure enough, Ariadna was no longer the quivering ruin but as beautiful as she had been as a girl. She was serene, her skin white, her pretty nose upturned, and those lush lips slightly opened as if expecting to be kissed by some dashing young officer.

This is how I'll remember her, thought Sashenka. What a beauty. Yet she felt a gnawing dissatisfaction and uneasiness: she had never known her. Her mother had been a stranger.

And who was she herself in this play? She no longer belonged there. While her mother was dying, she had become her daughter again. Her father, who had been unfazed by revolutions, wars, strikes and abdications, by his daughter's arrest, his brother's mischief, his wife's affairs, who had defied Petrograd workers, Baku assassins and aristocratic anti-Semites, had crumpled under this, a domestic suicide. He had abandoned his business, left his contracts unsigned, his contacts neglected and, in a few weeks, he had lost almost all interest in money. The businesses in Baku, Odessa and Tiflis were already unravelling because the Azeri Turks, Ukrainians and Georgians were liberating themselves from the Russian Empire. But the details were in his mind, and it seemed that this unshaven, grief-stricken man was beset by doubts about everything. She could hear him jabbering and crying.

It seemed to Sashenka that she might be losing both parents in one day.

She did not cry any more – she had cried often enough in recent nights – but still she longed to know why her mother had used her daughter's gun. Was Ariadna punishing Sashenka? Or was it simply the first weapon that had come to hand?

Sashenka stood beside the bed for a long time as people came and went to pay their respects. Gideon staggered into the room and kissed Ariadna's forehead. He ordered the doctor to sedate her father. The old Jews prayed. She watched as Turbin reclaimed the wicked she-devil of St Petersburg.

Ariadna's smile remained, but gradually her face started to subside. Her cheeks sank, and her gentile nose, the perfect little nose that had allowed her to romance Guards officers and English noblemen, became Semitic and hooked. Sashenka's grandfather covered the body with a white shroud, and lit two candles in silver candle-holders at the head of the bed. Miriam covered the mirrors with cloths and opened the windows. Since Zeitlin himself seemed paralysed, the rabbi took control. Orthodox Jews, liberated by the Revolution and allowed to visit the capital, appeared in this most secular of houses, as if by magic. Low stools were provided for the women to sit shiva.

There was a debate among the rabbis about what to do with the body. A suicide was beyond God's law and should have consigned her to an unholy burial, another tragedy for Ariadna's father. But two other rabbis had arrived and they asked what had actually killed Ariadna. An infection, Dr Gemp replied, not a bullet. By this pragmatic and merciful device, the Rabbi of Turbin was allowed to bury his daughter Finkel, known as Ariadna, in the Jewish cemetery.

Finally, the servants, shocked and confused by the presence of these gaberdine-coated Jews with ringlets and black hats, filed past the bed.

Sashenka knew she had to get back to her job at the Bolshevik newspaper. As if on cue, the door opened and Mendel, who had appeared only once for ten minutes a few days after the shooting, limped into the room between two young comrades, the powerful, thick-set Vanya Palitsyn, now clad in a leather coat and boots with a pistol in his holster, and the slim, virile Georgian, Satinov, who wore a sailor's jacket and boots. They brought the welcome breath of a new age into the chamber of decay.

Mendel was wearing a long lambskin coat and a worker's cap. He approached the bed, looked coldly at his sister's face for a moment, shook his head and then nodded at his sobbing parents.

'Mama, Papa!' he said, in his deep voice. 'I'm sorry.'

'Is that all you have to say to us?' asked Miriam through a curtain of tears. 'Mendel?'

'You've wasted enough time here, Comrade Zeitlin,' Mendel said brusquely to Sashenka. 'Comrade Lenin arrived last night at the Finland Station. I've got a job for you. Get your things. Let's go.'

'Wait, Comrade Mendel,' said Vanya Palitsyn quietly. 'She's lost a mother. Let her take her time.'

Mendel stopped. 'We've work to do and Bolsheviks can't and shouldn't have families. But if you say so . . .' He hesitated, looking back at his parents and the deathbed. 'I lost a sister too.'

'I'll bring Comrade Snowfox,' said Vanya Palitsyn. 'You two go ahead.'

Satinov kissed Sashenka thrice and hugged her – he was a Georgian after all, she remembered. 'You mourn all you need,' said Satinov, following Mendel as he limped out.

Vanya Palitsyn, brawny in his leathers and holster, looked out of place in the exquisite boudoir, yet Sashenka appreciated his support. She saw his brown eyes scan the room and imagined what the peasant-worker would make of the decadent trappings of capitalism: of all those dresses and jewels, Zeitlin the prostrate, sobbing industrialist, the society doctor in his cape, the half-soused bon viveur Gideon, the tearful servants and the rabbi. Vanya could not take his eyes off those wailing Jews from Poland!

Sashenka was pleased to be able to smile at something.

'I've read about deathbeds in Chekhov stories,' she said quietly to him, 'but I never realized they're so theatrical. Everyone has a role to play.'

Vanya just nodded, then he patted Sashenka on the shoulder. 'Don't rush, comrade,' he whispered. 'We'll wait. Cry all you need. Then go and get cleaned up, little fox,' said Vanya, his tenderness all the more touching in one so big. 'You'll come back for the funeral but for now I've got a motor car outside. I'm taking you to the mansion. I'll wait for you downstairs.'

Sashenka took in the room and the family in a last sweeping glance of farewell. She approached the bed and kissed her mother's forehead. She was crying again and she noticed tears in Vanya's eyes too.

'Vanya, wait. I'm coming right now,' said Sashenka, her voice breaking as she backed out of the room.

CHAPTER 39

At midday the next day, in the silk-walled splendour of the art-deco Kschessinskaya Mansion, where once the ballerina Mathilde had entertained both her Romanov lovers, Sashenka sat at an Underwood typewriter at a neat wooden desk on the first floor. She wore a white blouse, buttoned to the neck, a long brown woollen skirt and sensible laced-up ankle boots. She was not alone in the anteroom. Three other girls, two of them wearing round spectacles, also sat at desks, pivoting round to watch the door.

The mansion was manned by armed Red Guards, actually workers who wore parts of different uniforms, commanded by Vanya himself. Vanya had taken her out for a quick meal the night before and driven her home afterwards. In the morning she had visited, for the first and last time, the Moorish-style synagogue on Lermontovskaya (which her father had paid for) and then seen her mother buried in the Jewish cemetery, where she, her father and Uncle Gideon seemed drowned in the sea of mourning Jews in their wide hats and coats, attired entirely in black, except for the white fringes of their prayer shawls.

Vanya had begged her to take another day off but she replied that her mother had already consumed too many days of her life, and she'd hurried back to her new office – to meet her new boss. How could a young person wish to be anywhere else in the world but here in the ballerina's mansion, the furnace of revolution, the cynosure of history?

At her desk, Sashenka heard the buzz of excitement from downstairs. The meeting in the ballroom, attended by all the Central Committee, was about to break up. Just then its doors opened, the sounds of laughter and voices and the tread of boots on the stairs coming closer.

Sashenka and the other three girls settled their bottoms on their chairs and straightened their blouses, and arranged their inkwells and blotters once again.

The smoked-glass doors flew open.

'Well, Illich, here's your new office. Your assistants are all waiting for you, ready to get to work.' Mendel stepped into the room with Comrade Zinoviev, a scruffy Jewish man in a tweed jacket with a frizzy shock of black hair, and Stalin, a small, wiry, moustachioed Georgian wearing a naval jacket and baggy trousers tucked into soft boots.

They stopped at her desk: Zinoviev's nervous eyes scanned Sashenka's bosom and skirts while

Comrade Stalin, smiling slightly, looked searchingly into her face with eyes the colour of speckled honey. Georgians had a charming way of looking at women, she thought.

The men seemed to be borne on a wave of energy and enthusiasm. Zinoviev smelt of cognac; Stalin reeked of tobacco. He was carrying an unlit pipe in his left hand, a burning cigarette in the corner of his mouth. They turned as a short, squat man with a bald bulging forehead, neat reddish beard and a very bourgeois three-piece suit with tie and watch chain burst into the room. In one hand he held a bowler hat and in the other a wad of newspapers and he was talking relentlessly and hoarsely in a well-educated voice.

'Good work, Comrade Mendel,' said Lenin, looking at Sashenka and the others with his twinkling, slanted eyes. 'This all looks fine. Where's my office? Ah yes, through there.' The desk was ready, paper, inkwell and a telephone. 'Mendel, which is your niece, the one who studied at the Smolny?'

'That's me, comrade!' said Sashenka, standing up and almost curtsying. 'Comrade Zeitlin.'

'A Bolshevik from the Smolny, eh? Did you really have to bow to the Empress every morning? Well, well, we represent the workers of the world – but we're not prejudiced against a decent education, are we, comrades?'

Lenin laughed merrily as he headed towards the glass double doors of his office, then turned briskly, smiling no more. 'Right, ladies, henceforth you're working for me. We're not waiting for power to fall into our laps. We're going to take power ourselves and smash our enemies into the dust. You're to be available for work at all times. Often you'll need to sleep in the office. Make arrangements accordingly. No smoking in this office!'

He pointed at Sashenka. 'All right, come on in, Comrade Zeitlin, I shall I start with you. I've got an article to dictate. Let's go!'

A NOTE ON NAMES AND LANGUAGE

Places in Russia tend to change their names with the tides of history. St Petersburg was founded by Peter the Great in 1703 and was known as such until 1914, when Nicholas II changed its Germanic sound to Petrograd, 'Peter's city'. In 1924, the Bolsheviks renamed it Leningrad. In 1991 it became St Petersburg once again. Tiflis is now known as Tbilisi, the capital of independent Georgia.

The rulers of Russia were called Tsars, though in 1721 Peter the Great declared himself Emperor and thenceforth the Romanovs were known as both.

Russians use three names in a formal context: a first name, a patronymic (meaning son/daughter of) and a surname. Thus Sashenka's formal name is Alexandra Samuilovna Zeitlin and Vanya is Ivan Nikolaievich Palitsyn. But Russians (and Georgians) usually also use diminutives as nick-names: Sashenka is the diminutive of Alexandra and Vanya is the diminutive of Ivan, etc.

In the Pale of Settlement, the Jews spoke Yiddish

as their vernacular, prayed in Hebrew and petitioned in Russian. The Georgian language is totally different from Russian and has its own alphabet and literature.